SNOOPY™

BOOGIE DOWN!

Other *Peanuts* Kids' Collections

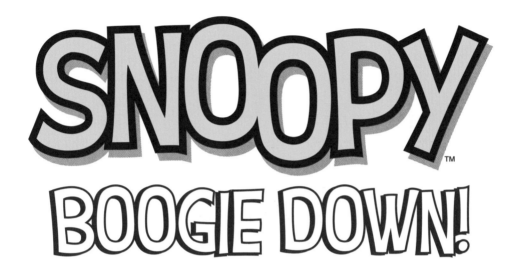

SNOOPY ™
BOOGIE DOWN!

A **PEANUTS** ™ Collection

CHARLES M. SCHULZ

Andrews McMeel
PUBLISHING®

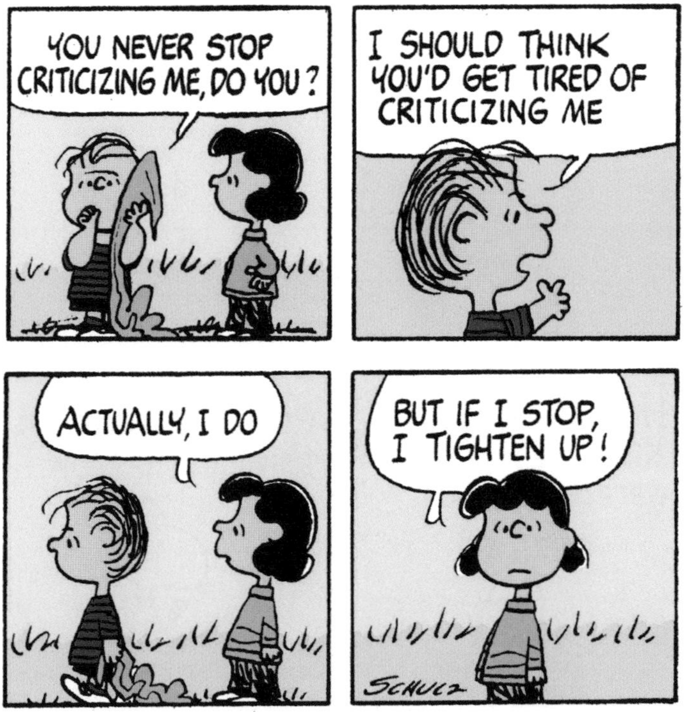
YOU NEVER STOP CRITICIZING ME, DO YOU?
I SHOULD THINK YOU'D GET TIRED OF CRITICIZING ME
ACTUALLY, I DO
BUT IF I STOP, I TIGHTEN UP!
SCHULZ

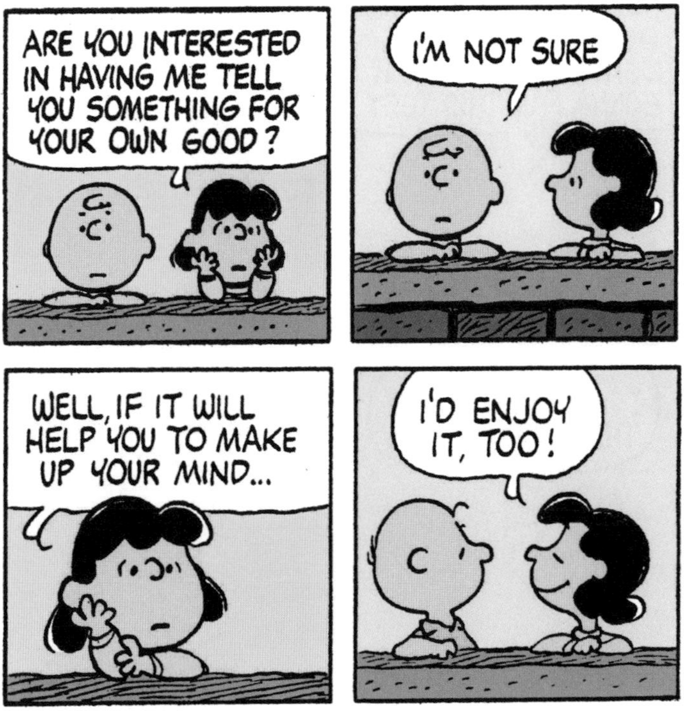
ARE YOU INTERESTED IN HAVING ME TELL YOU SOMETHING FOR YOUR OWN GOOD?
I'M NOT SURE
WELL, IF IT WILL HELP YOU TO MAKE UP YOUR MIND...
I'D ENJOY IT, TOO!

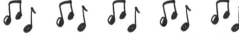

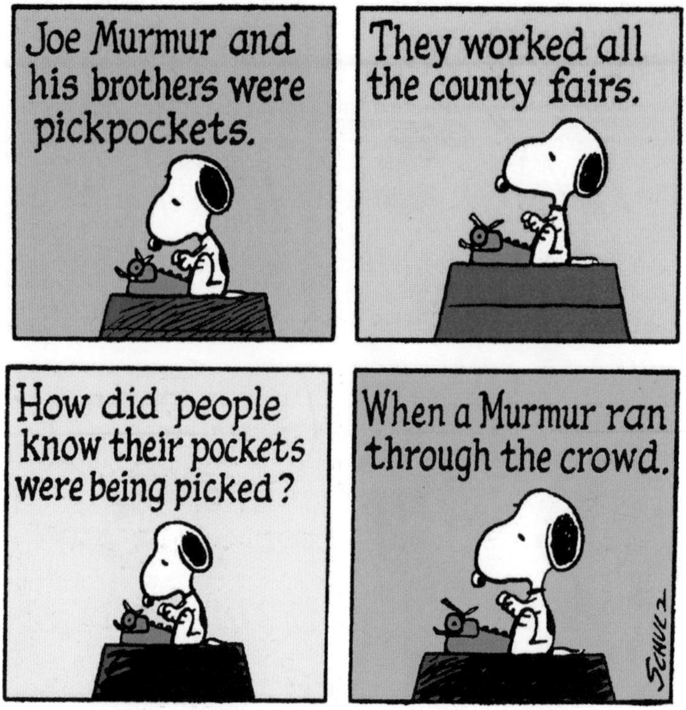
Joe Murmur and his brothers were pickpockets.
They worked all the county fairs.
How did people know their pockets were being picked?
When a Murmur ran through the crowd.
SCHULZ

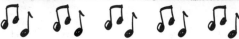

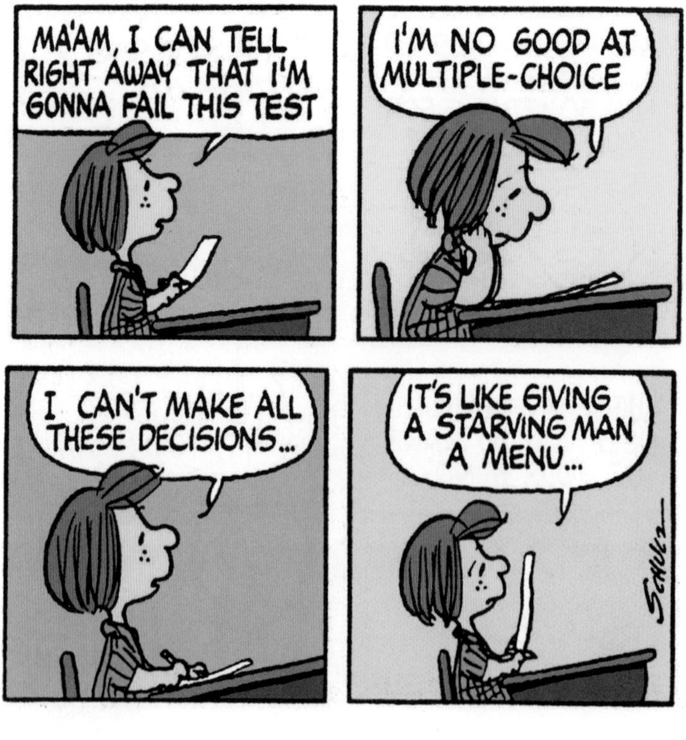
MA'AM, I CAN TELL RIGHT AWAY THAT I'M GONNA FAIL THIS TEST
I'M NO GOOD AT MULTIPLE-CHOICE
I CAN'T MAKE ALL THESE DECISIONS...
IT'S LIKE GIVING A STARVING MAN A MENU...
SCHULZ

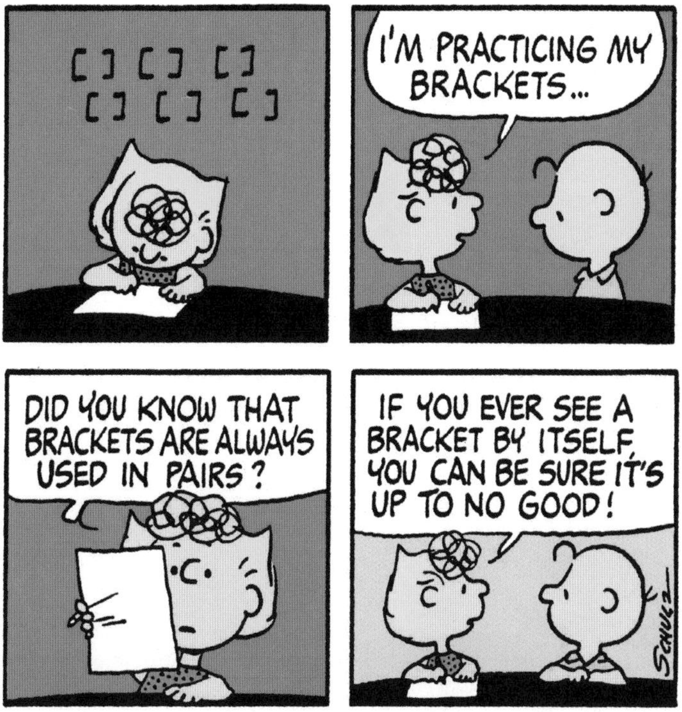
I'M PRACTICING MY BRACKETS...
DID YOU KNOW THAT BRACKETS ARE ALWAYS USED IN PAIRS?
IF YOU EVER SEE A BRACKET BY ITSELF, YOU CAN BE SURE IT'S UP TO NO GOOD!
SCHULZ

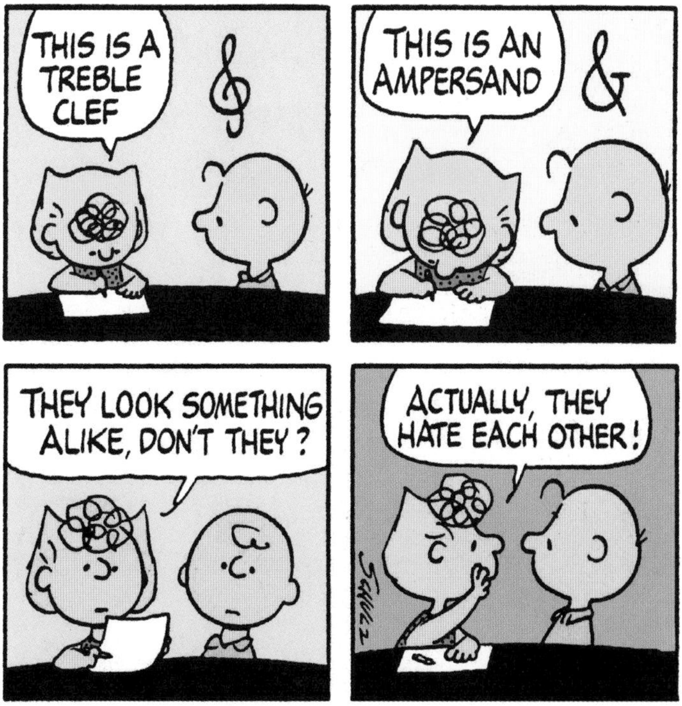
THIS IS A TREBLE CLEF
THIS IS AN AMPERSAND
THEY LOOK SOMETHING ALIKE, DON'T THEY?
ACTUALLY, THEY HATE EACH OTHER!
SCHULZ

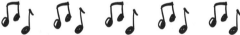

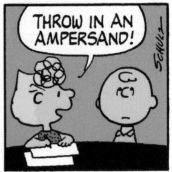

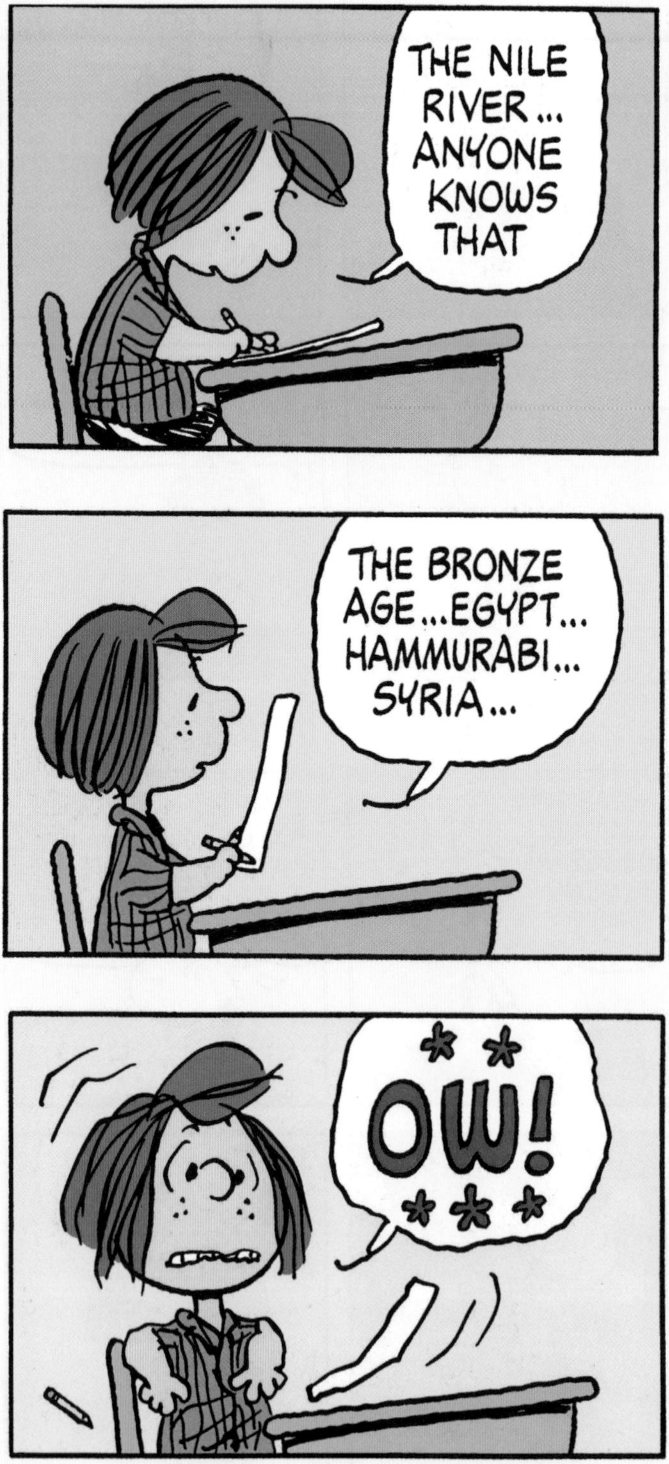
THE NILE RIVER... ANYONE KNOWS THAT
THE BRONZE AGE...EGYPT... HAMMURABI... SYRIA...
OW!

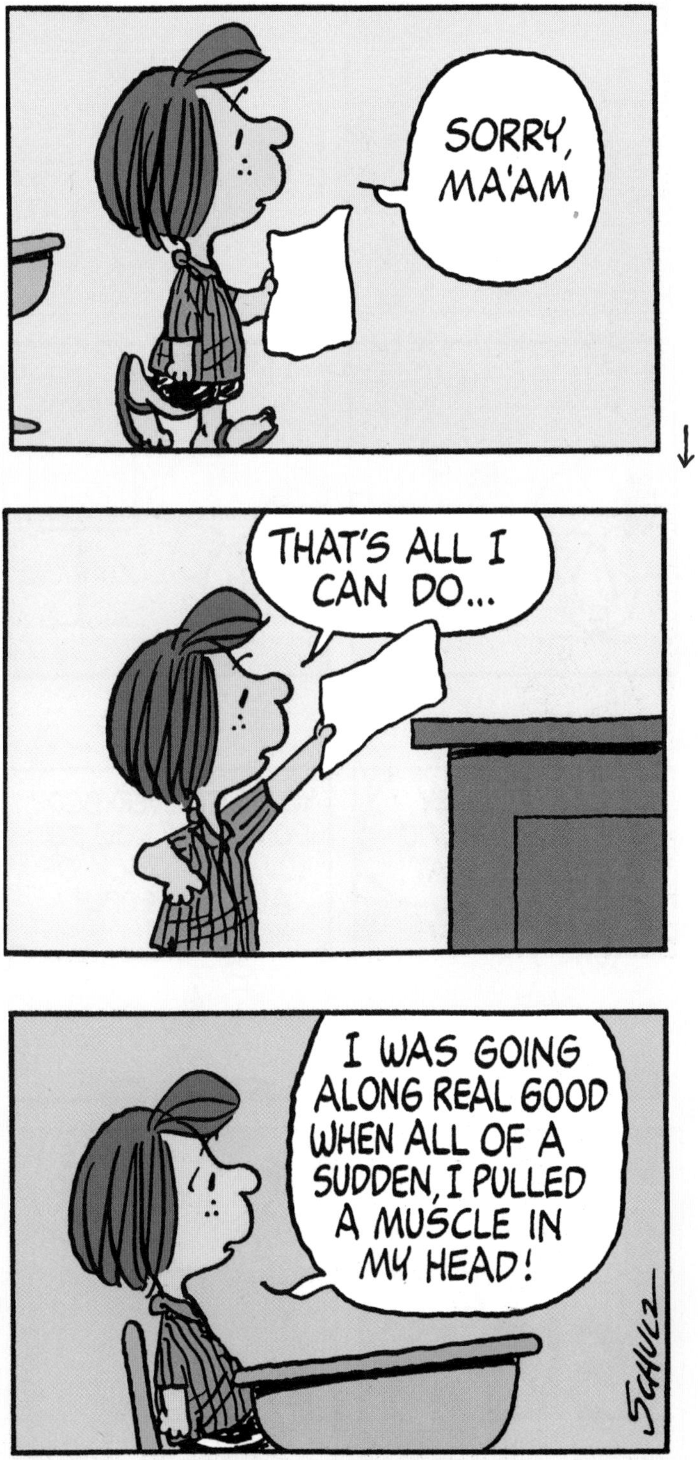
SORRY, MA'AM
THAT'S ALL I CAN DO...
I WAS GOING ALONG REAL GOOD WHEN ALL OF A SUDDEN, I PULLED A MUSCLE IN MY HEAD!
SCHULZ

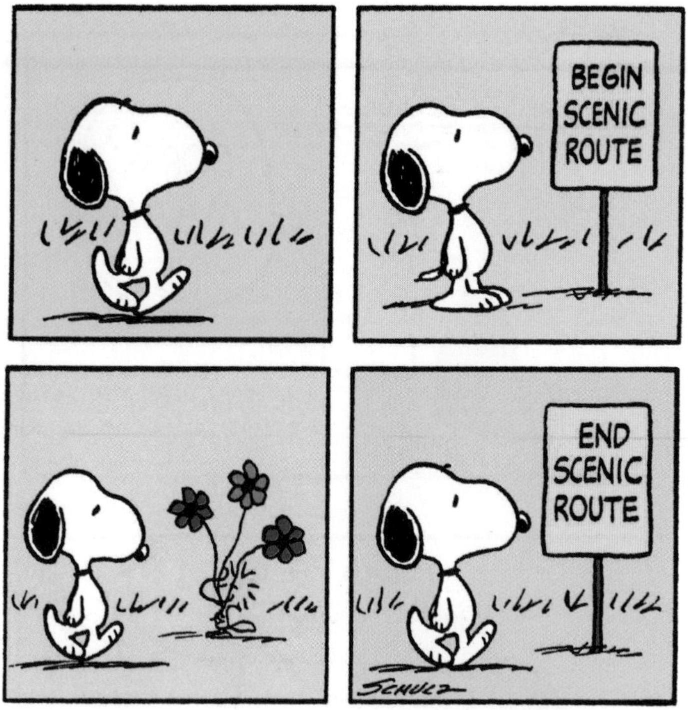
BEGIN SCENIC ROUTE
END SCENIC ROUTE
SCHULZ

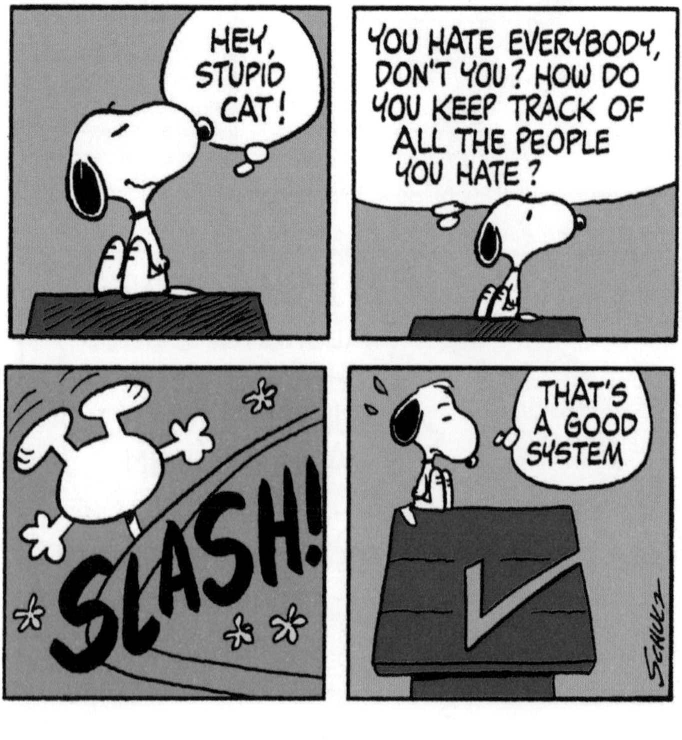
HEY, STUPID CAT!
YOU HATE EVERYBODY, DON'T YOU? HOW DO YOU KEEP TRACK OF ALL THE PEOPLE YOU HATE?
SLASH!
THAT'S A GOOD SYSTEM
SCHULZ

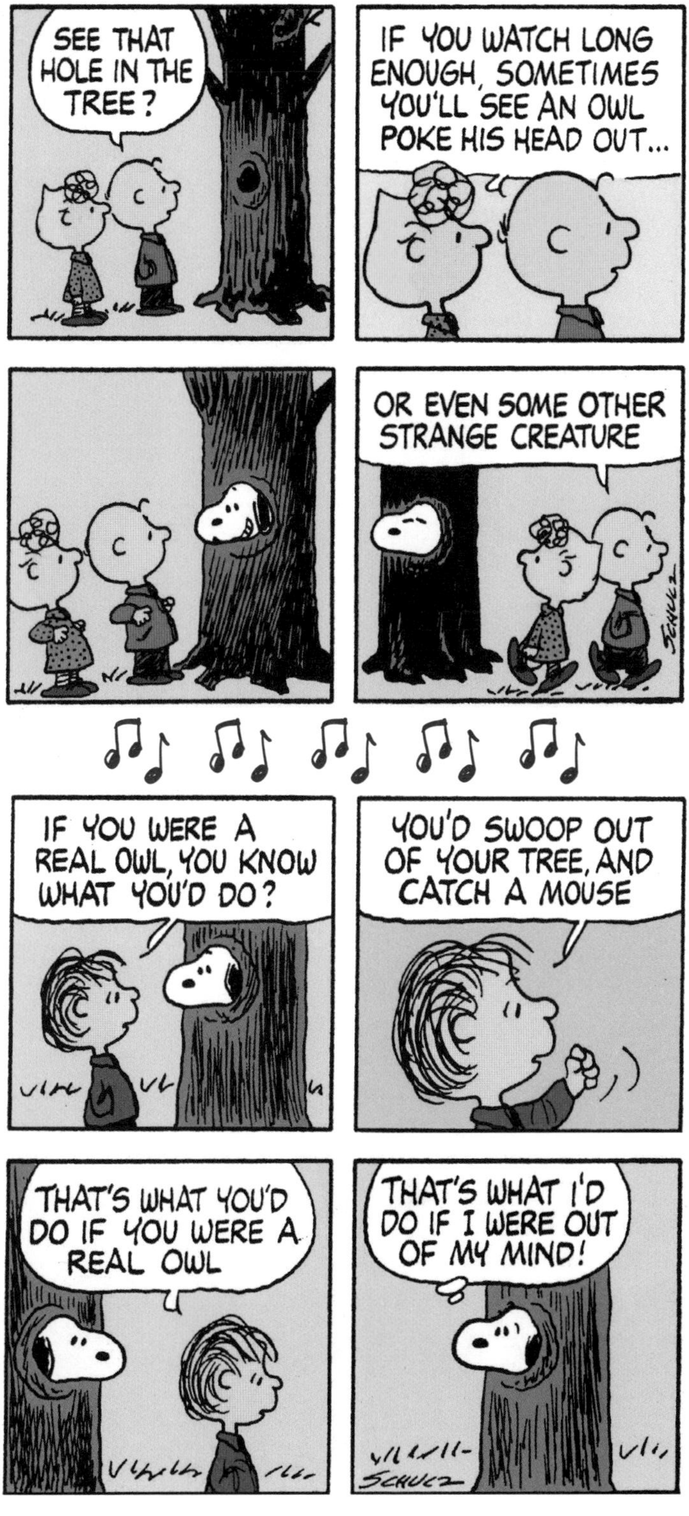
SEE THAT HOLE IN THE TREE?
IF YOU WATCH LONG ENOUGH, SOMETIMES YOU'LL SEE AN OWL POKE HIS HEAD OUT...
OR EVEN SOME OTHER STRANGE CREATURE
SCHULZ
IF YOU WERE A REAL OWL, YOU KNOW WHAT YOU'D DO?
YOU'D SWOOP OUT OF YOUR TREE, AND CATCH A MOUSE
THAT'S WHAT YOU'D DO IF YOU WERE A REAL OWL
THAT'S WHAT I'D DO IF I WERE OUT OF MY MIND!
SCHULZ

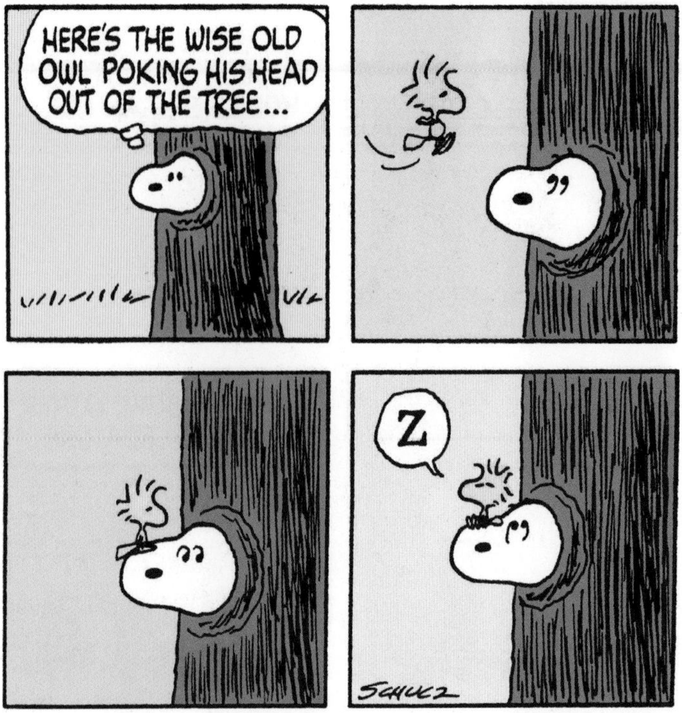
HERE'S THE WISE OLD OWL POKING HIS HEAD OUT OF THE TREE...
Z
SCHULZ

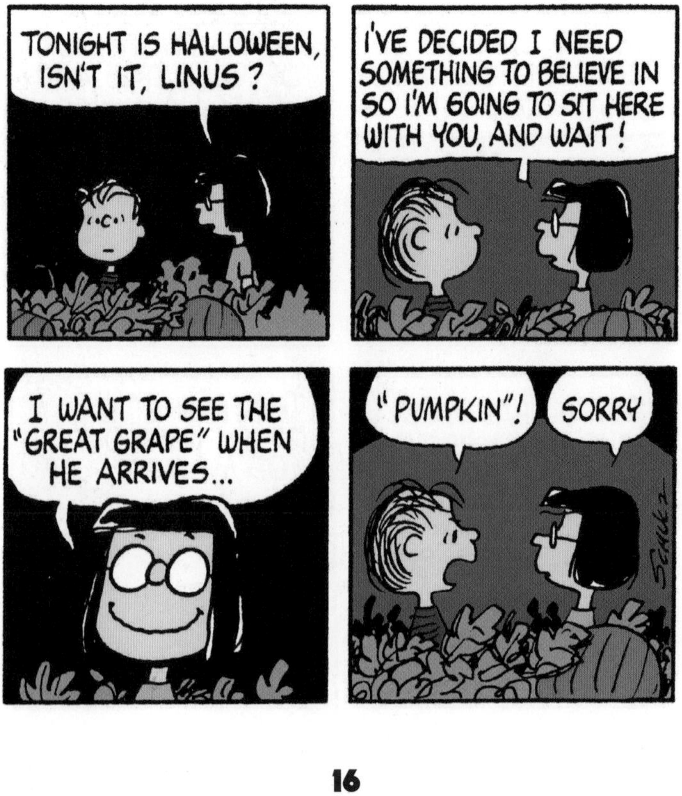
TONIGHT IS HALLOWEEN, ISN'T IT, LINUS ?
I'VE DECIDED I NEED SOMETHING TO BELIEVE IN SO I'M GOING TO SIT HERE WITH YOU, AND WAIT !
I WANT TO SEE THE "GREAT GRAPE" WHEN HE ARRIVES...
"PUMPKIN"!
SORRY
SCHULZ

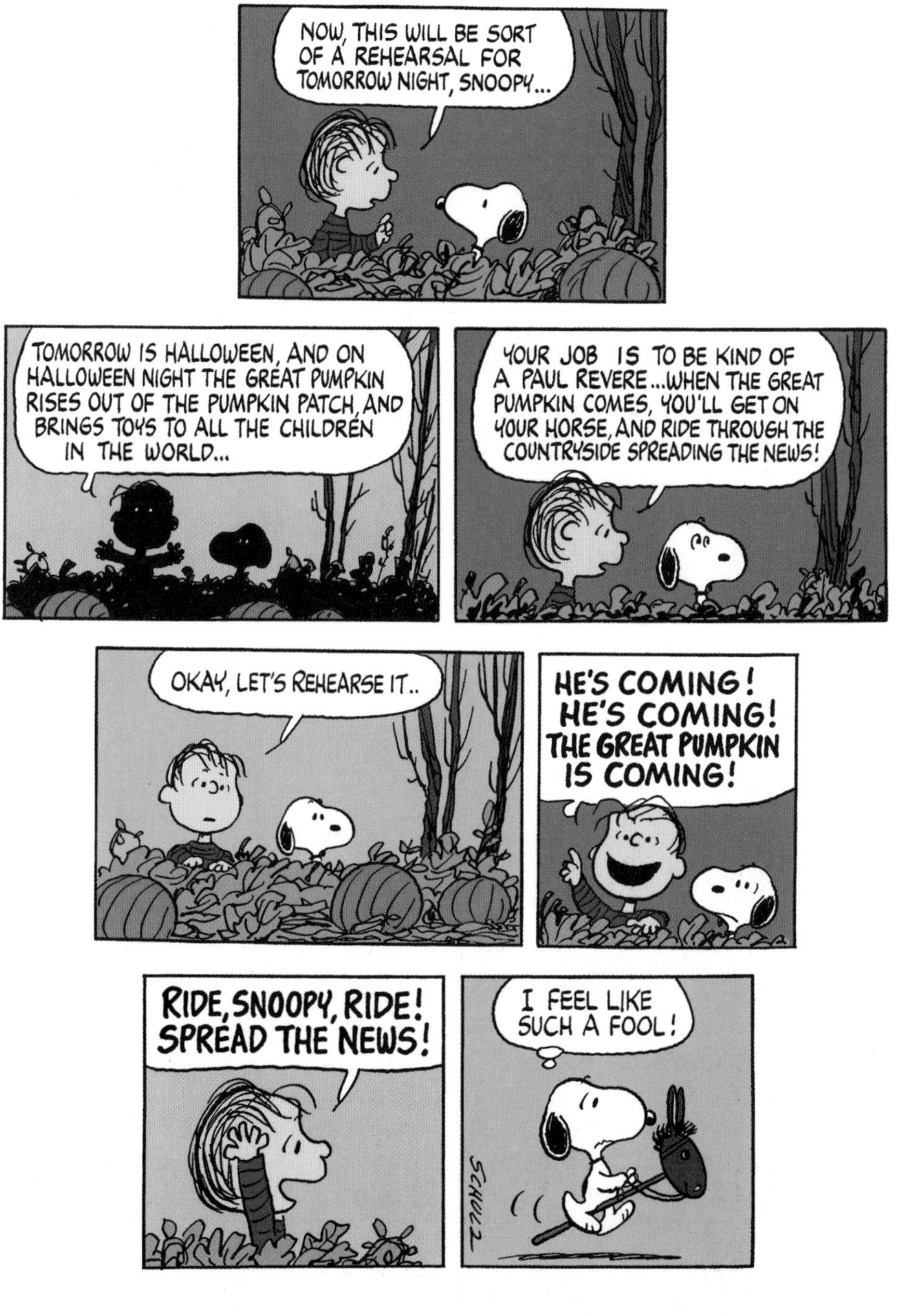
NOW, THIS WILL BE SORT OF A REHEARSAL FOR TOMORROW NIGHT, SNOOPY...
TOMORROW IS HALLOWEEN, AND ON HALLOWEEN NIGHT THE GREAT PUMPKIN RISES OUT OF THE PUMPKIN PATCH, AND BRINGS TOYS TO ALL THE CHILDREN IN THE WORLD...
YOUR JOB IS TO BE KIND OF A PAUL REVERE...WHEN THE GREAT PUMPKIN COMES, YOU'LL GET ON YOUR HORSE, AND RIDE THROUGH THE COUNTRYSIDE SPREADING THE NEWS!
OKAY, LET'S REHEARSE IT..
HE'S COMING! HE'S COMING! THE GREAT PUMPKIN IS COMING!
RIDE, SNOOPY, RIDE! SPREAD THE NEWS!
I FEEL LIKE SUCH A FOOL!
SCHULZ

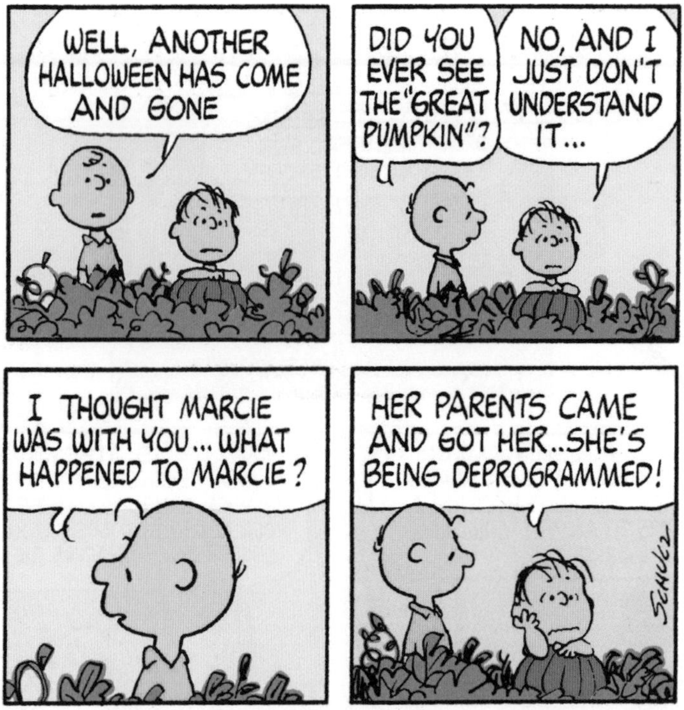
WELL, ANOTHER HALLOWEEN HAS COME AND GONE
DID YOU EVER SEE THE "GREAT PUMPKIN"?
NO, AND I JUST DON'T UNDERSTAND IT...
I THOUGHT MARCIE WAS WITH YOU... WHAT HAPPENED TO MARCIE?
HER PARENTS CAME AND GOT HER..SHE'S BEING DEPROGRAMMED!

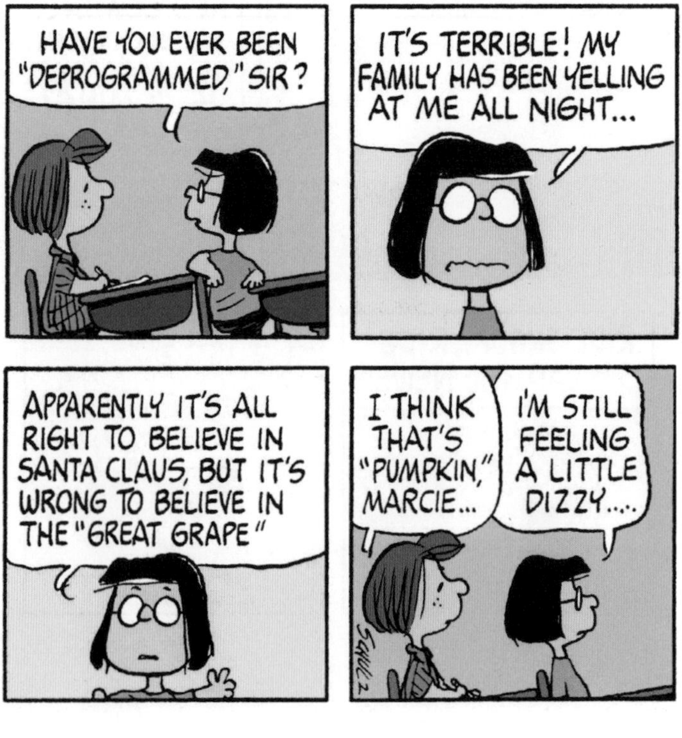
HAVE YOU EVER BEEN "DEPROGRAMMED," SIR?
IT'S TERRIBLE! MY FAMILY HAS BEEN YELLING AT ME ALL NIGHT...
APPARENTLY IT'S ALL RIGHT TO BELIEVE IN SANTA CLAUS, BUT IT'S WRONG TO BELIEVE IN THE "GREAT GRAPE"
I THINK THAT'S "PUMPKIN," MARCIE...
I'M STILL FEELING A LITTLE DIZZY.....

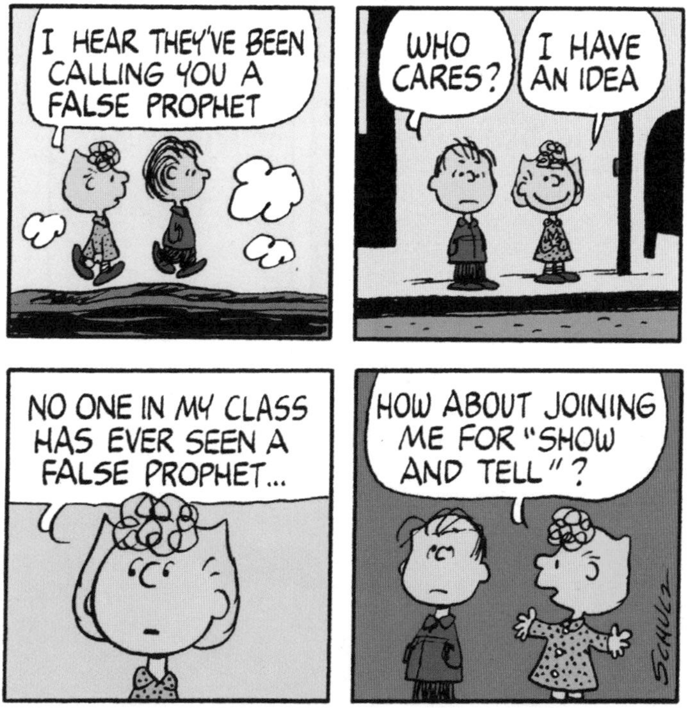
I HEAR THEY'VE BEEN CALLING YOU A FALSE PROPHET
WHO CARES?
I HAVE AN IDEA
NO ONE IN MY CLASS HAS EVER SEEN A FALSE PROPHET...
HOW ABOUT JOINING ME FOR "SHOW AND TELL"?

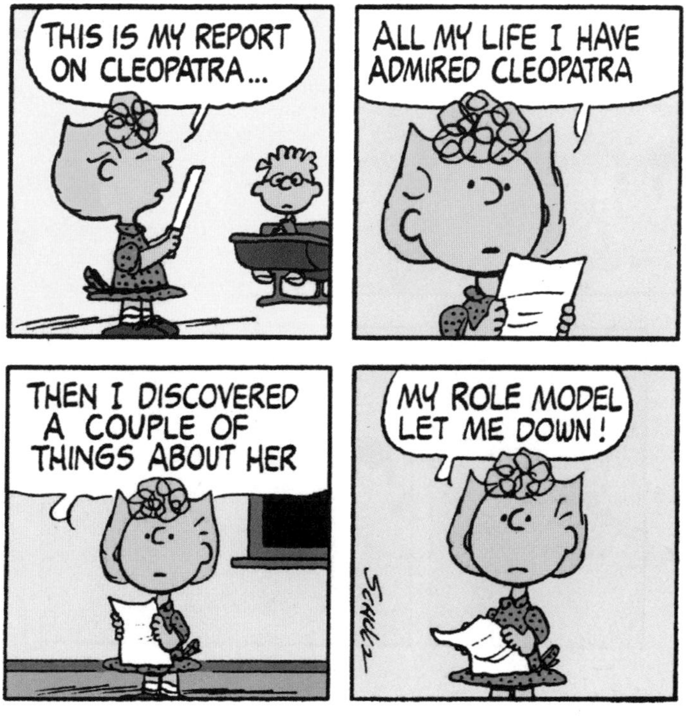
THIS IS MY REPORT ON CLEOPATRA...
ALL MY LIFE I HAVE ADMIRED CLEOPATRA
THEN I DISCOVERED A COUPLE OF THINGS ABOUT HER
MY ROLE MODEL LET ME DOWN!

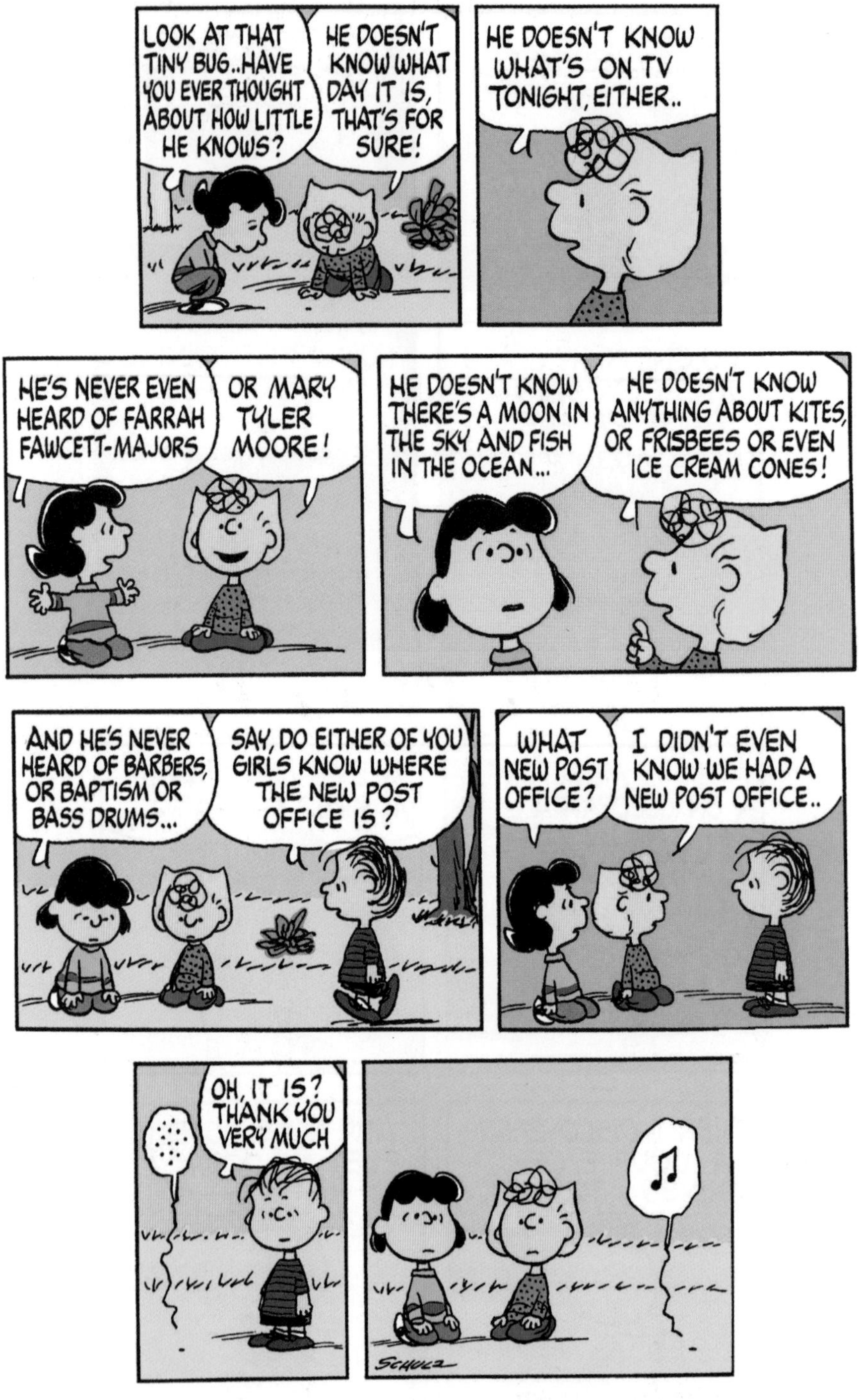
LOOK AT THAT TINY BUG..HAVE YOU EVER THOUGHT ABOUT HOW LITTLE HE KNOWS?
HE DOESN'T KNOW WHAT DAY IT IS, THAT'S FOR SURE!
HE DOESN'T KNOW WHAT'S ON TV TONIGHT, EITHER..
HE'S NEVER EVEN HEARD OF FARRAH FAWCETT-MAJORS
OR MARY TYLER MOORE!
HE DOESN'T KNOW THERE'S A MOON IN THE SKY AND FISH IN THE OCEAN...
HE DOESN'T KNOW ANYTHING ABOUT KITES, OR FRISBEES OR EVEN ICE CREAM CONES!
AND HE'S NEVER HEARD OF BARBERS, OR BAPTISM OR BASS DRUMS...
SAY, DO EITHER OF YOU GIRLS KNOW WHERE THE NEW POST OFFICE IS?
WHAT NEW POST OFFICE?
I DIDN'T EVEN KNOW WE HAD A NEW POST OFFICE..
OH, IT IS? THANK YOU VERY MUCH
SCHULZ

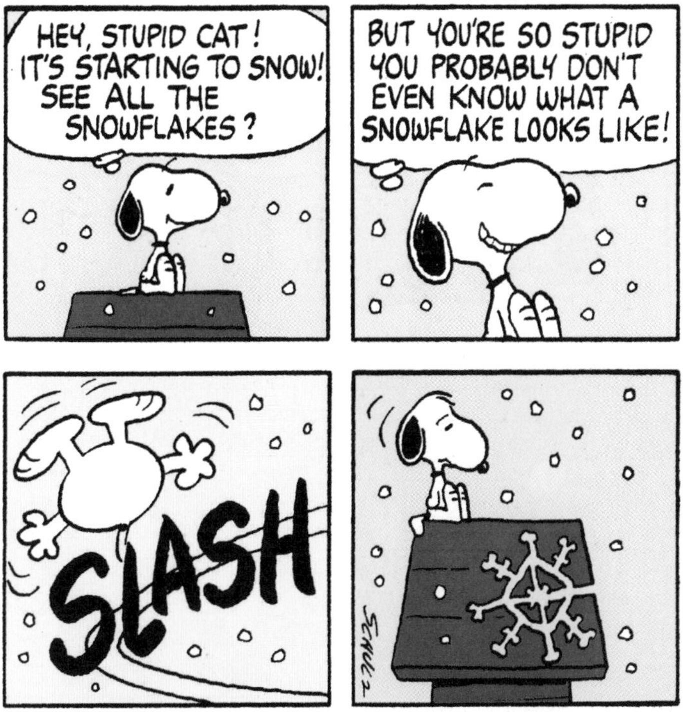
HEY, STUPID CAT! IT'S STARTING TO SNOW! SEE ALL THE SNOWFLAKES?
BUT YOU'RE SO STUPID YOU PROBABLY DON'T EVEN KNOW WHAT A SNOWFLAKE LOOKS LIKE!
SLASH
SCHULZ

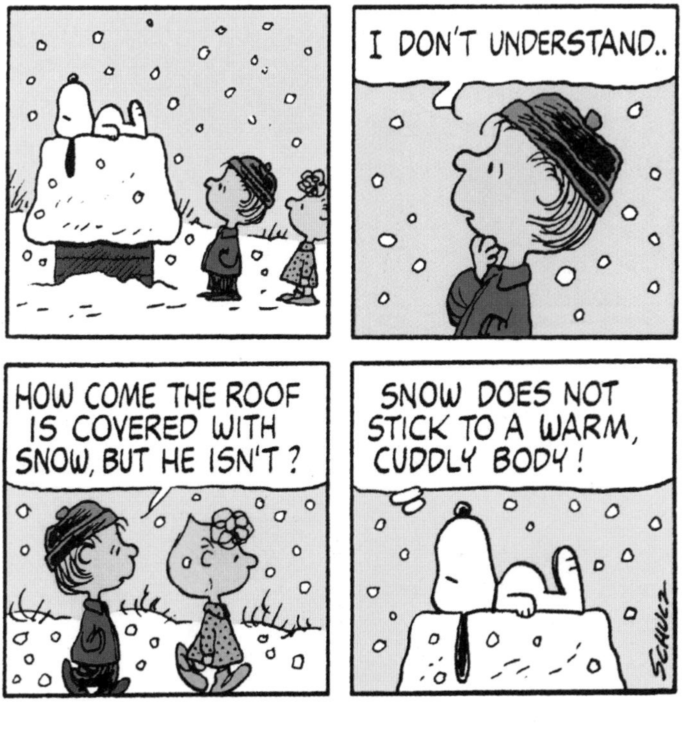
I DON'T UNDERSTAND..
HOW COME THE ROOF IS COVERED WITH SNOW, BUT HE ISN'T?
SNOW DOES NOT STICK TO A WARM, CUDDLY BODY!
SCHULZ

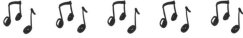

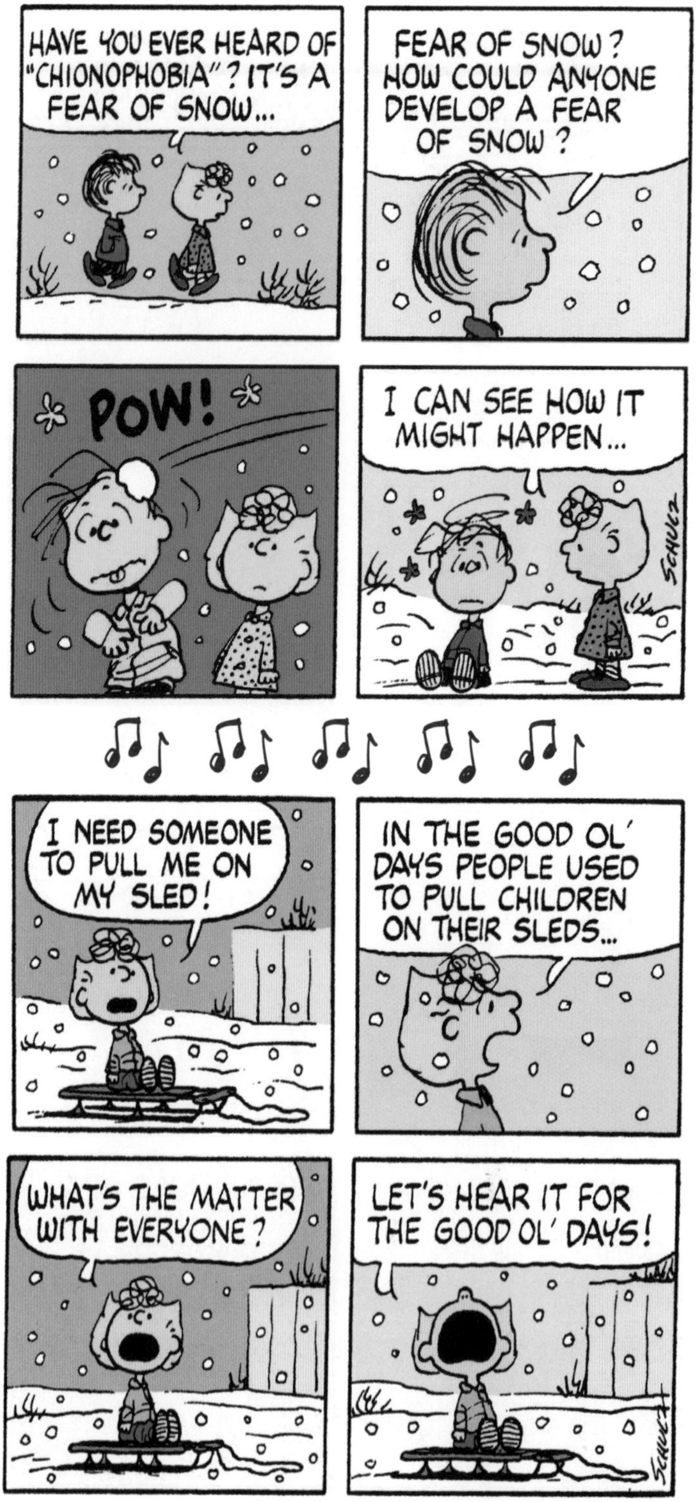
HAVE YOU EVER HEARD OF "CHIONOPHOBIA"? IT'S A FEAR OF SNOW...
FEAR OF SNOW? HOW COULD ANYONE DEVELOP A FEAR OF SNOW?
POW!
I CAN SEE HOW IT MIGHT HAPPEN...
SCHULZ
I NEED SOMEONE TO PULL ME ON MY SLED!
IN THE GOOD OL' DAYS PEOPLE USED TO PULL CHILDREN ON THEIR SLEDS...
WHAT'S THE MATTER WITH EVERYONE?
LET'S HEAR IT FOR THE GOOD OL' DAYS!
SCHULZ

BAM BAM BAM
SORRY...WE'RE CLOSED FOR REMODELING!
SLAM!
SCARED YOU, DIDN'T I ?
SCHULZ
BAM BAM BAM
I'M SORRY... YOUR SUPPER ISN'T READY
WE'VE BEEN HAVING A FEW PROBLEMS LATELY
OUR COMPUTER BROKE DOWN!
SCHULZ

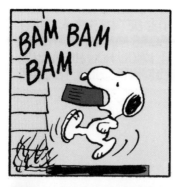

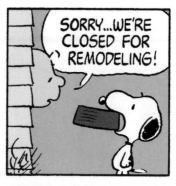

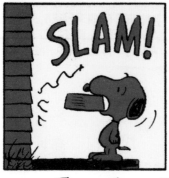

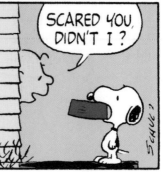

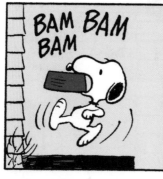

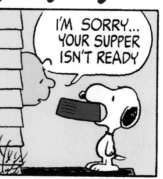

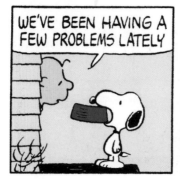

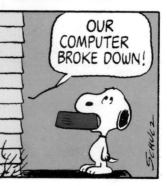

I'LL HOLD THE BALL, CHARLIE BROWN, AND YOU COME RUNNING UP AND KICK IT!

OH, SURE! WHAT YOU REALLY MEAN IS YOU'LL PULL IT AWAY, AND I'LL KILL MYSELF!

I HAVE A TIP FOR YOU, CHARLIE BROWN...JUST WATCH MY EYES...

YOUR EYES?

THAT'S RIGHT! YOU CAN ALWAYS TELL WHAT A PERSON IS GOING TO DO BY WATCHING THEIR EYES!

THAT'S A GOOD TIP... WATCH THE EYES... I SHOULD HAVE THOUGHT OF THAT BEFORE...

THIS YEAR I'M GONNA KICK THAT BALL OUT OF THE UNIVERSE!

AUGH!!

WUMP!

※ SIGH ※

SCHULZ

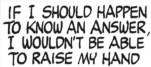

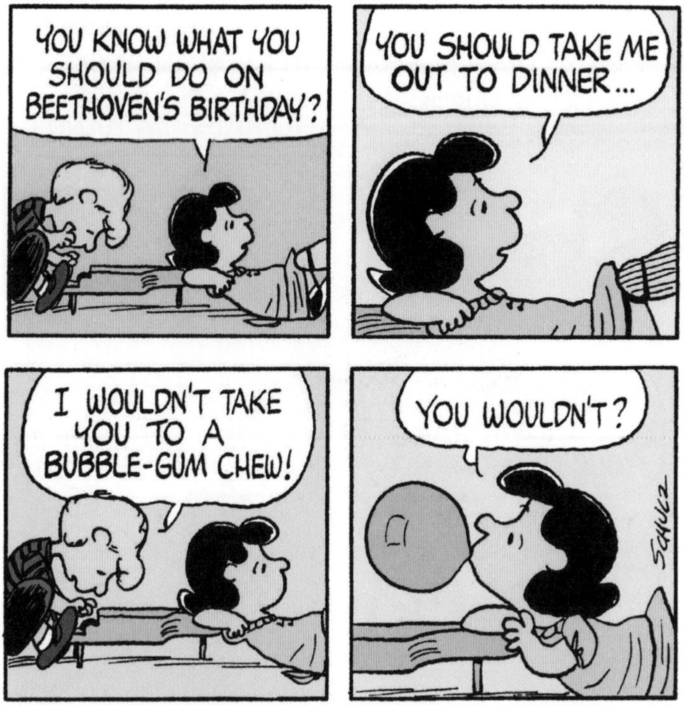
YOU KNOW WHAT YOU SHOULD DO ON BEETHOVEN'S BIRTHDAY?
YOU SHOULD TAKE ME OUT TO DINNER...
I WOULDN'T TAKE YOU TO A BUBBLE-GUM CHEW!
YOU WOULDN'T?
SCHULZ

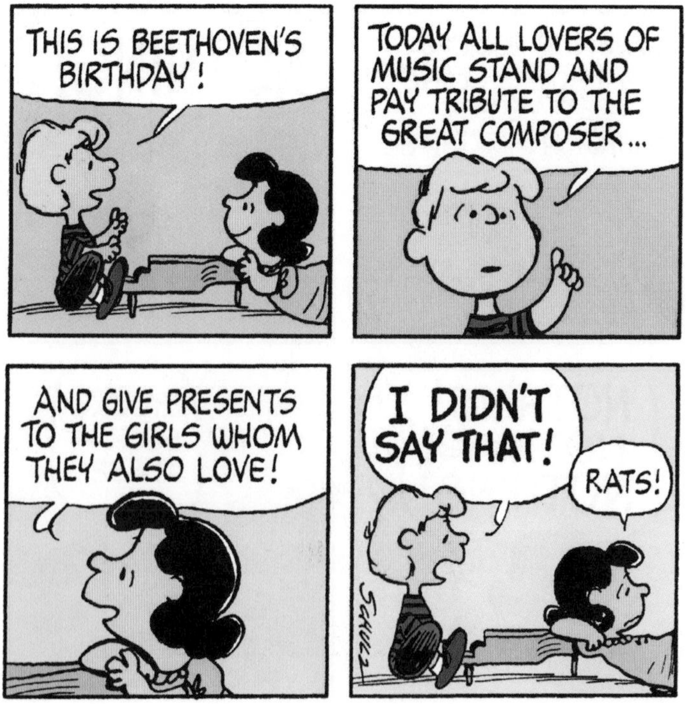
THIS IS BEETHOVEN'S BIRTHDAY!
TODAY ALL LOVERS OF MUSIC STAND AND PAY TRIBUTE TO THE GREAT COMPOSER...
AND GIVE PRESENTS TO THE GIRLS WHOM THEY ALSO LOVE!
I DIDN'T SAY THAT!
RATS!
SCHULZ

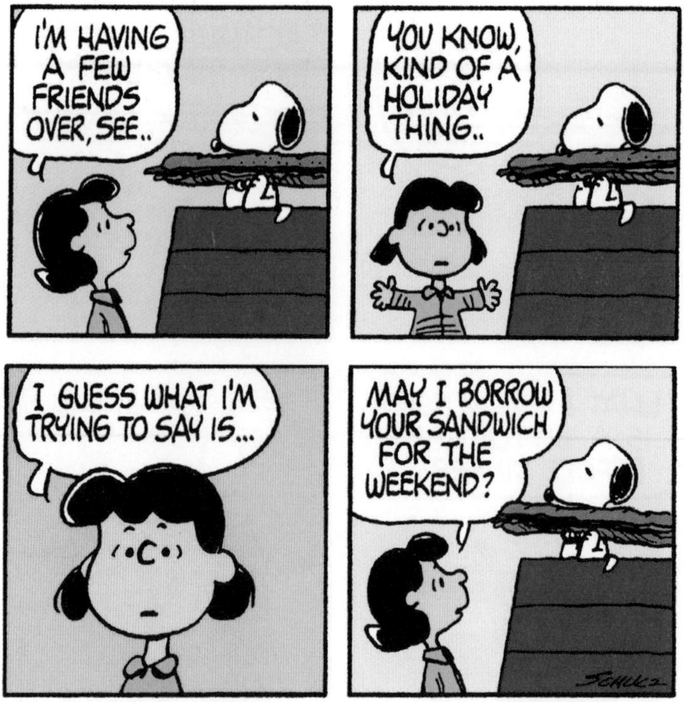
I'M HAVING A FEW FRIENDS OVER, SEE..
YOU KNOW, KIND OF A HOLIDAY THING..
I GUESS WHAT I'M TRYING TO SAY IS...
MAY I BORROW YOUR SANDWICH FOR THE WEEKEND?

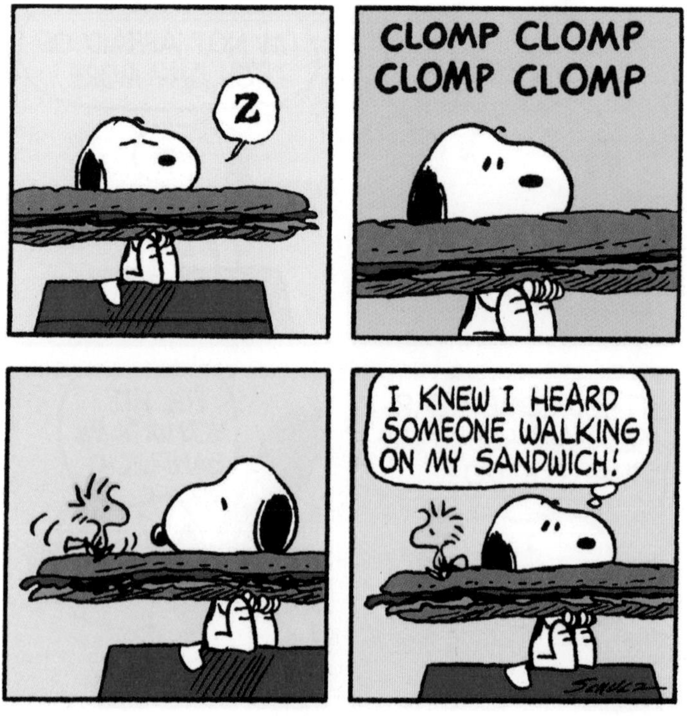
Z
CLOMP CLOMP
CLOMP CLOMP
I KNEW I HEARD SOMEONE WALKING ON MY SANDWICH!

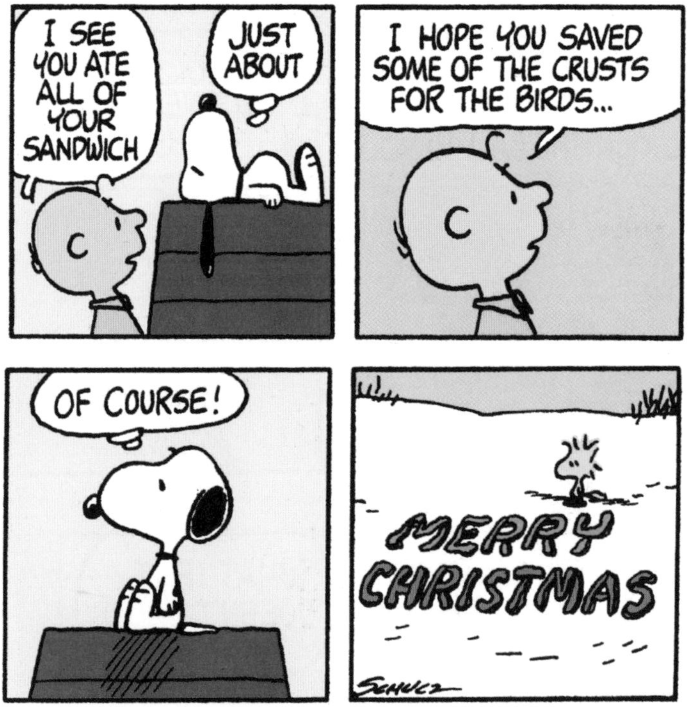
I SEE YOU ATE ALL OF YOUR SANDWICH
JUST ABOUT
I HOPE YOU SAVED SOME OF THE CRUSTS FOR THE BIRDS...
OF COURSE!
MERRY CHRISTMAS
SCHULZ

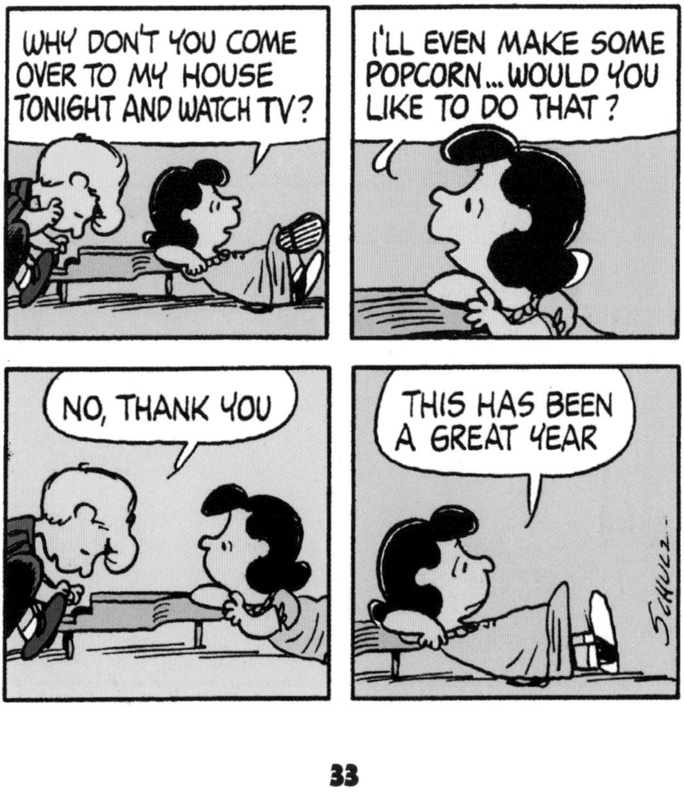
WHY DON'T YOU COME OVER TO MY HOUSE TONIGHT AND WATCH TV?
I'LL EVEN MAKE SOME POPCORN...WOULD YOU LIKE TO DO THAT?
NO, THANK YOU
THIS HAS BEEN A GREAT YEAR
SCHULZ

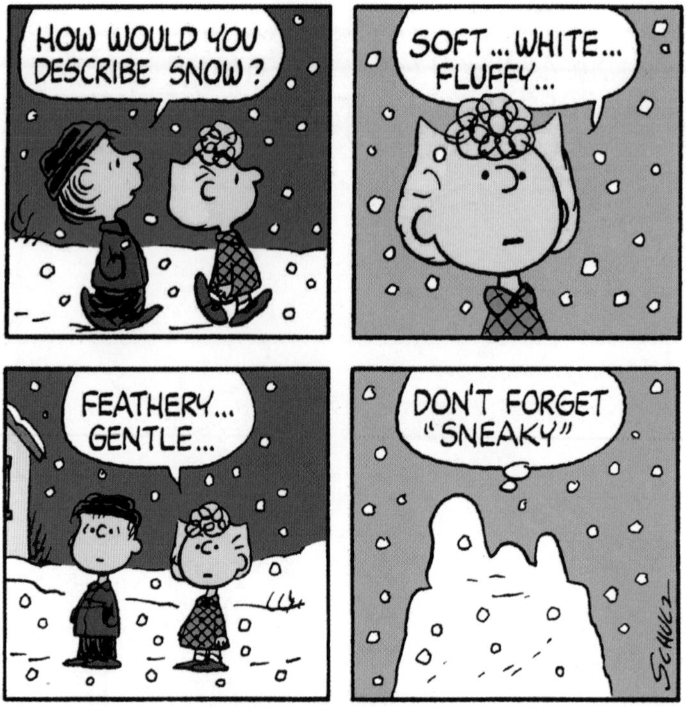
HOW WOULD YOU DESCRIBE SNOW?
SOFT...WHITE... FLUFFY...
FEATHERY... GENTLE...
DON'T FORGET "SNEAKY"
SCHULZ

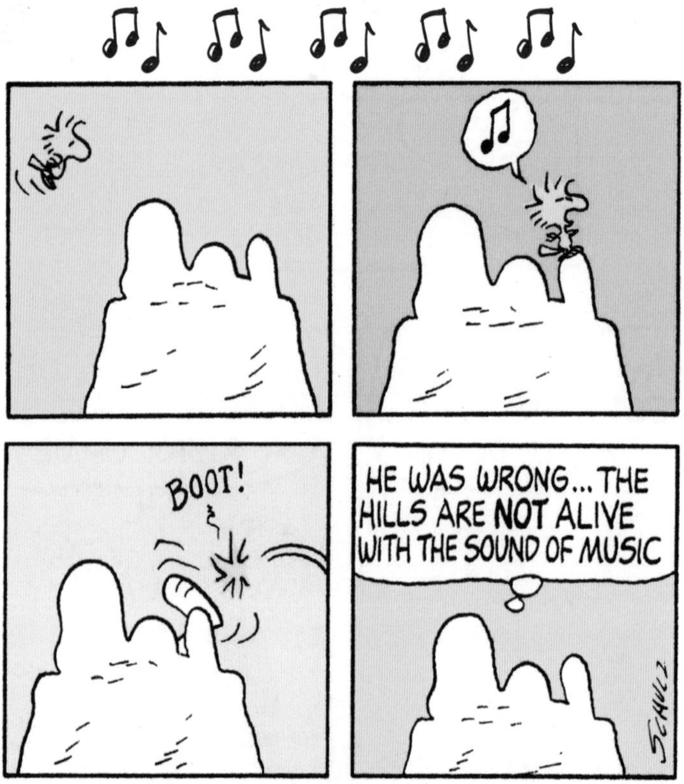
BOOT!
HE WAS WRONG...THE HILLS ARE **NOT** ALIVE WITH THE SOUND OF MUSIC
SCHULZ

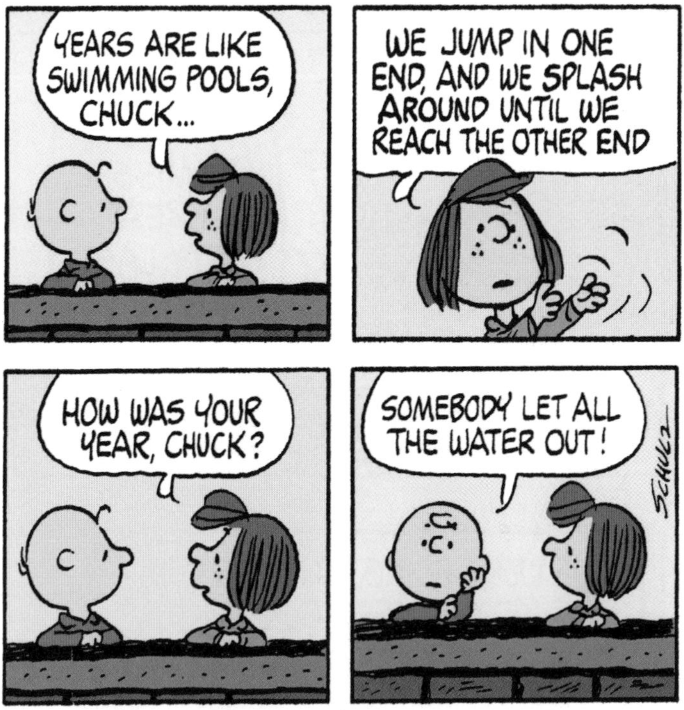
YEARS ARE LIKE SWIMMING POOLS, CHUCK...
WE JUMP IN ONE END, AND WE SPLASH AROUND UNTIL WE REACH THE OTHER END
HOW WAS YOUR YEAR, CHUCK?
SOMEBODY LET ALL THE WATER OUT!
SCHULZ

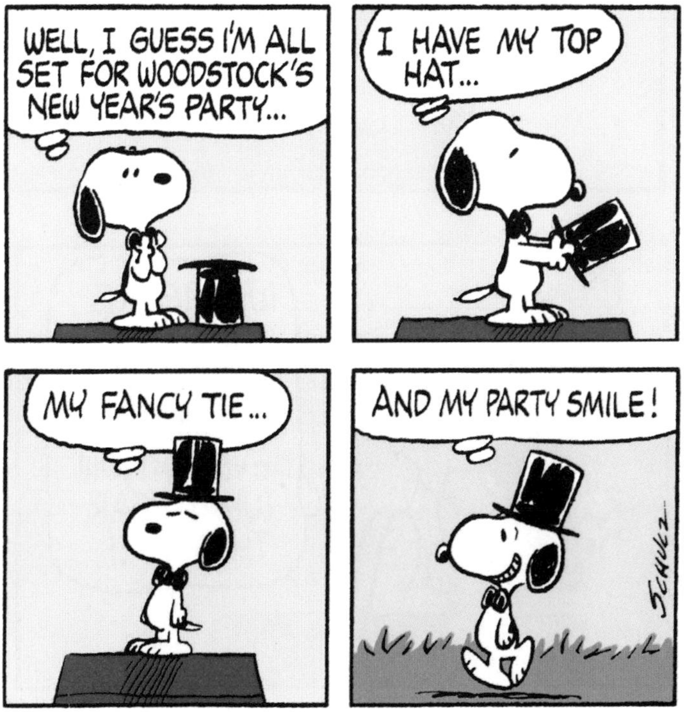
WELL, I GUESS I'M ALL SET FOR WOODSTOCK'S NEW YEAR'S PARTY...
I HAVE MY TOP HAT...
MY FANCY TIE...
AND MY PARTY SMILE!
SCHULZ

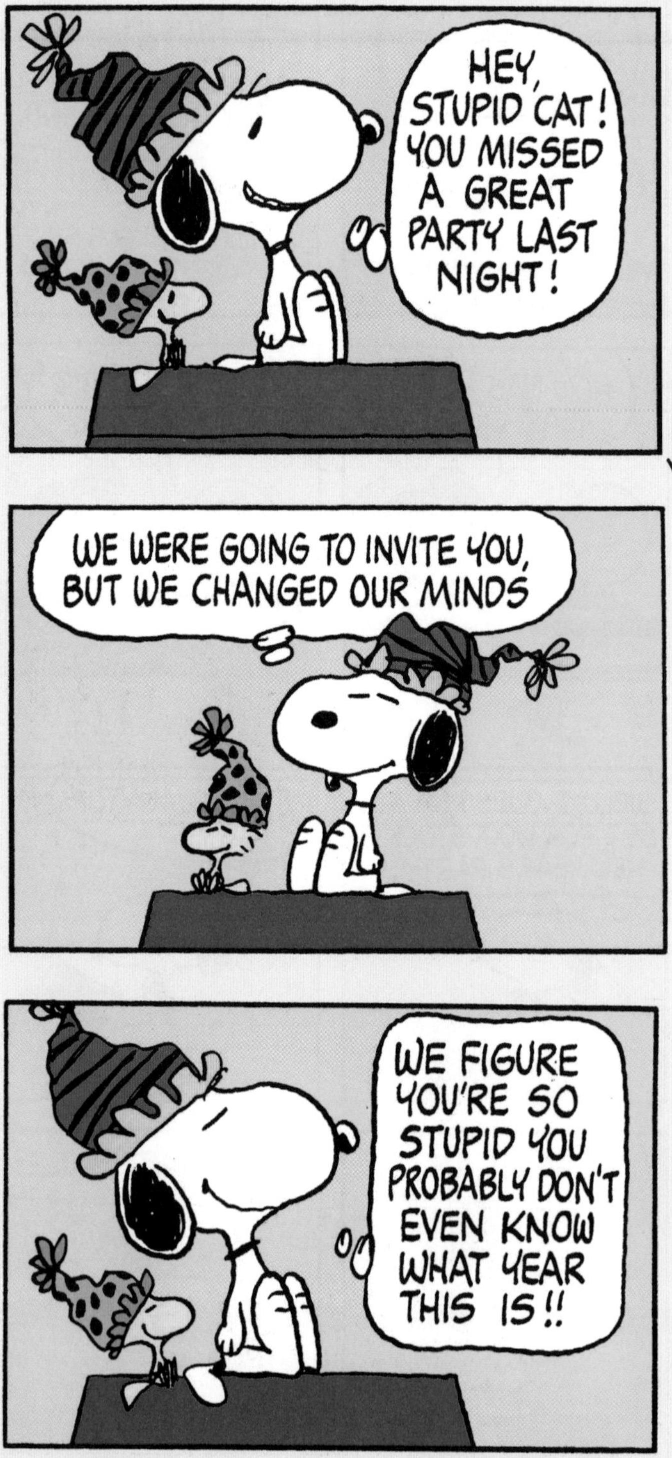
HEY, STUPID CAT! YOU MISSED A GREAT PARTY LAST NIGHT!
WE WERE GOING TO INVITE YOU, BUT WE CHANGED OUR MINDS
WE FIGURE YOU'RE SO STUPID YOU PROBABLY DON'T EVEN KNOW WHAT YEAR THIS IS!!

WHAT DO YOU THINK OF MY FORWARD LOOPS, COACH?
GROWL, SNARL, SNAP, GROWF, BARK, WOOF!
ARE ALL SKATING COACHES AS CRABBY AS YOU?
GROWL, SNARL, SNAP, GROWF, BARK, WOOF!
SCHULZ

HOW MANY SKATING TESTS ARE THERE, SIR?
EIGHT, MARCIE, AND THEY GET HARDER AND HARDER
SOMETIMES I THINK THE ONLY THING THAT KEEPS ME GOING IS THE ENCOURAGING WORDS OF MY COACH...
GROWL, SNARL, SNAP, GROWF, BARK, WOOF!
SCHULZ

OKAY, BEAUTIFUL, GET OFF THE ICE!! WE'RE GONNA PLAY HOCKEY!

HOCKEY?! GET LOST, NECKHEAD! I WAS HERE FIRST!!

YOU WOULDN'T LIKE TO GET HIT WITH A HOCKEY STICK WOULD YOU, BEAUTIFUL?

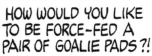

HOW WOULD YOU LIKE TO BE FORCE-FED A PAIR OF GOALIE PADS?!

LISTEN, BEAUTIFUL, GET YOUR STUPID FIGURE SKATES OFF THE ICE! WE WANNA PLAY HOCKEY, SEE?

WE HAVE TEN HOCKEY STICKS HERE TELLING YOU TO "GET OFF THE ICE!"

OH, YEAH? COME ON AND TRY SOMETHING! ME AND MY COACH'LL TAKE YOU ALL ON!!

I THINK I'LL GO HOME.. I HAVE SOME CHAIN LETTERS TO WRITE...

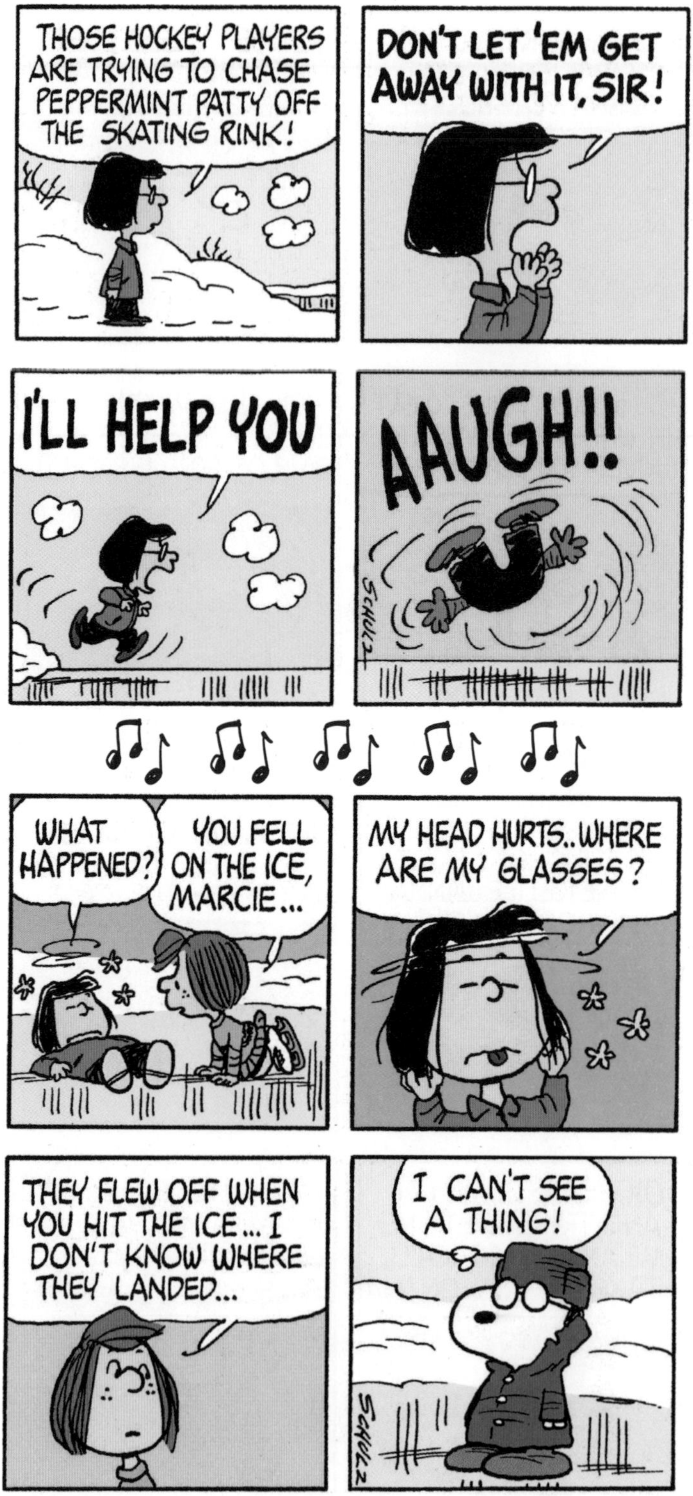
THOSE HOCKEY PLAYERS ARE TRYING TO CHASE PEPPERMINT PATTY OFF THE SKATING RINK!
DON'T LET 'EM GET AWAY WITH IT, SIR!
I'LL HELP YOU
AAUGH!!
SCHULZ
WHAT HAPPENED?
YOU FELL ON THE ICE, MARCIE...
MY HEAD HURTS..WHERE ARE MY GLASSES?
THEY FLEW OFF WHEN YOU HIT THE ICE... I DON'T KNOW WHERE THEY LANDED...
I CAN'T SEE A THING!
SCHULZ

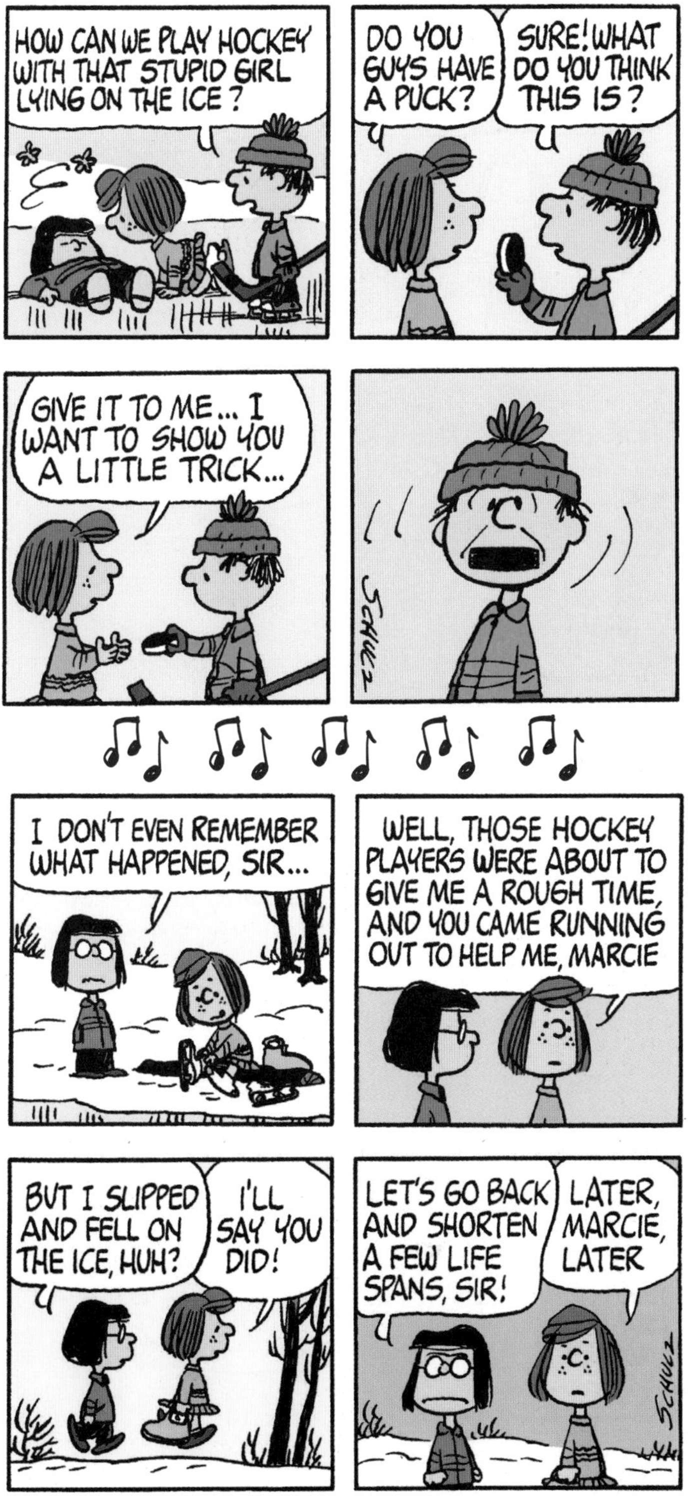
HOW CAN WE PLAY HOCKEY WITH THAT STUPID GIRL LYING ON THE ICE?
DO YOU GUYS HAVE A PUCK?
SURE! WHAT DO YOU THINK THIS IS?
GIVE IT TO ME... I WANT TO SHOW YOU A LITTLE TRICK...
SCHULZ
I DON'T EVEN REMEMBER WHAT HAPPENED, SIR...
WELL, THOSE HOCKEY PLAYERS WERE ABOUT TO GIVE ME A ROUGH TIME, AND YOU CAME RUNNING OUT TO HELP ME, MARCIE
BUT I SLIPPED AND FELL ON THE ICE, HUH?
I'LL SAY YOU DID!
LET'S GO BACK AND SHORTEN A FEW LIFE SPANS, SIR!
LATER, MARCIE, LATER
SCHULZ

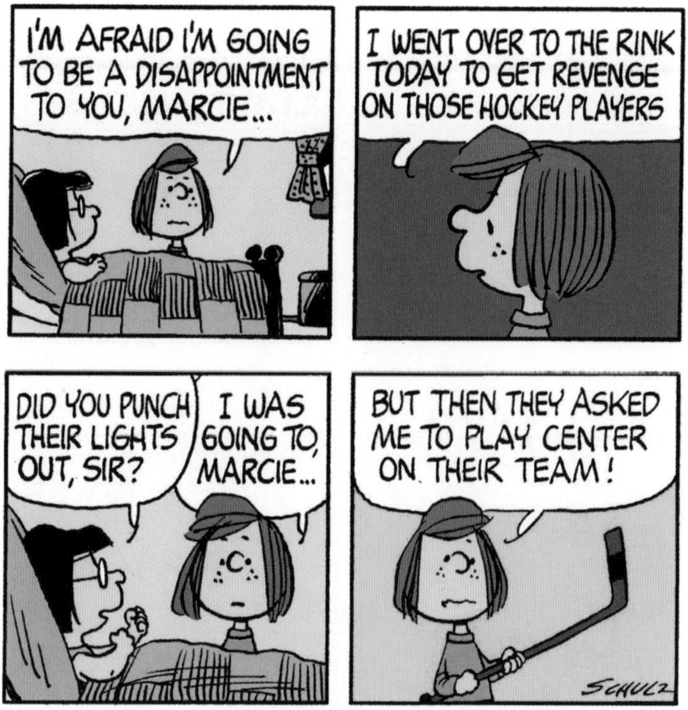
I'M AFRAID I'M GOING TO BE A DISAPPOINTMENT TO YOU, MARCIE...
I WENT OVER TO THE RINK TODAY TO GET REVENGE ON THOSE HOCKEY PLAYERS
DID YOU PUNCH THEIR LIGHTS OUT, SIR?
I WAS GOING TO, MARCIE...
BUT THEN THEY ASKED ME TO PLAY CENTER ON THEIR TEAM!
SCHULZ

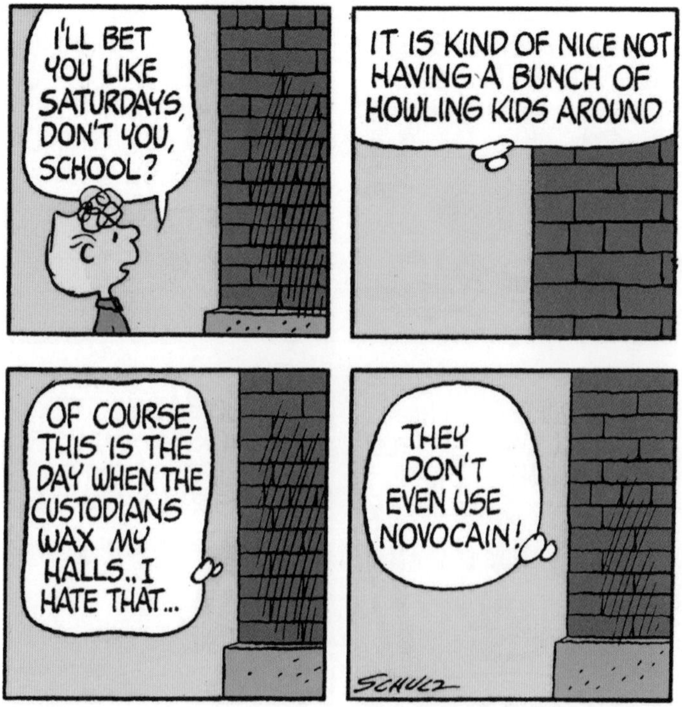
I'LL BET YOU LIKE SATURDAYS, DON'T YOU, SCHOOL?
IT IS KIND OF NICE NOT HAVING A BUNCH OF HOWLING KIDS AROUND
OF COURSE, THIS IS THE DAY WHEN THE CUSTODIANS WAX MY HALLS.. I HATE THAT...
THEY DON'T EVEN USE NOVOCAIN!
SCHULZ

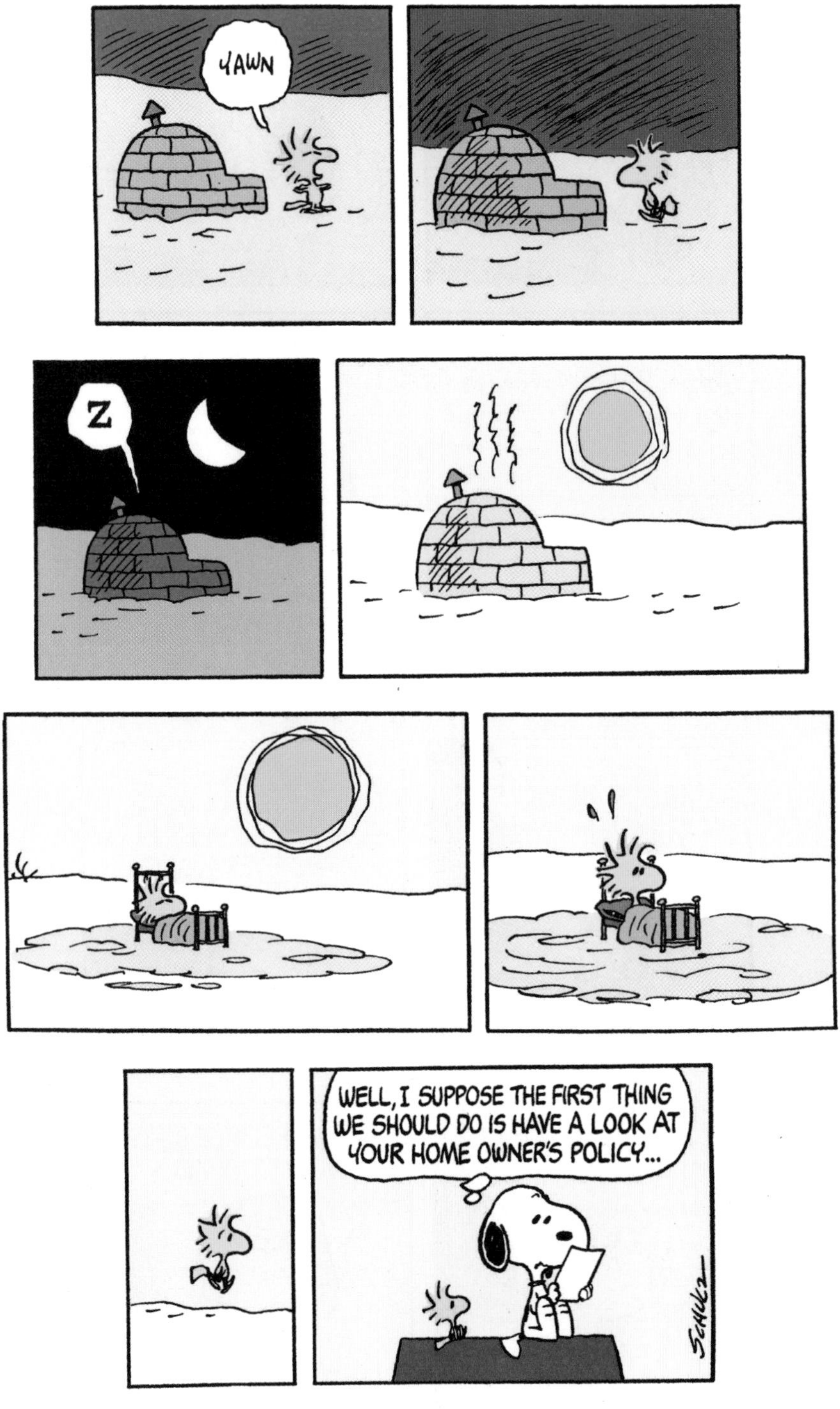
YAWN
Z
WELL, I SUPPOSE THE FIRST THING WE SHOULD DO IS HAVE A LOOK AT YOUR HOME OWNER'S POLICY...
SCHULZ

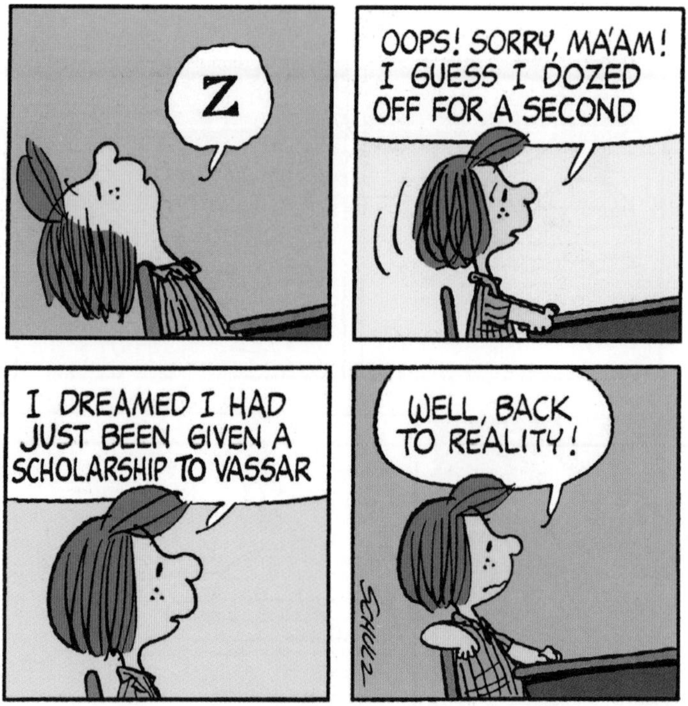
Z
OOPS! SORRY, MA'AM! I GUESS I DOZED OFF FOR A SECOND
I DREAMED I HAD JUST BEEN GIVEN A SCHOLARSHIP TO VASSAR
WELL, BACK TO REALITY!
SCHULZ

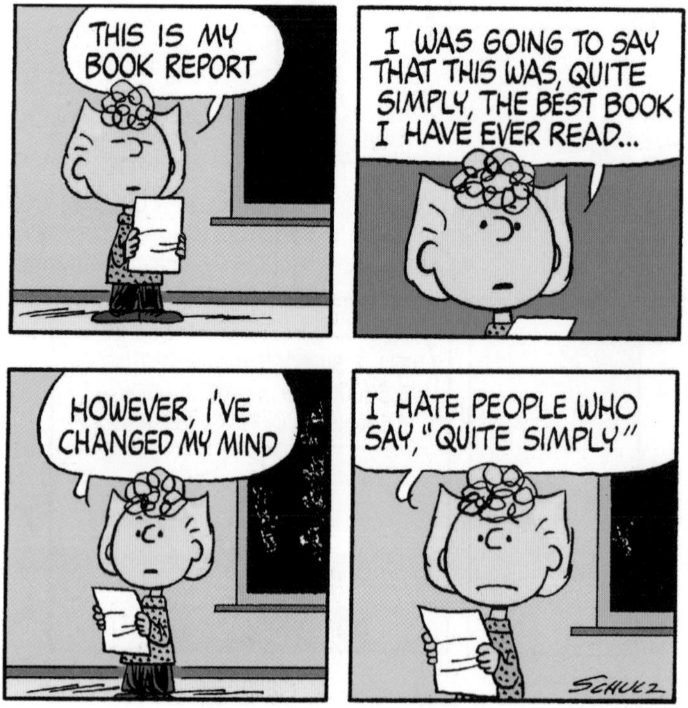
THIS IS MY BOOK REPORT
I WAS GOING TO SAY THAT THIS WAS, QUITE SIMPLY, THE BEST BOOK I HAVE EVER READ...
HOWEVER, I'VE CHANGED MY MIND
I HATE PEOPLE WHO SAY, "QUITE SIMPLY"
SCHULZ

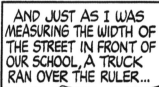

TODAY I'M GOING TO TEACH YOU HOW TO CATCH A FORWARD PASS...

ALL RIGHT, START RUNNING!

GET WAY OUT! WAY OUT!

BONK!

OKAY, NOW HERE'S WHAT YOU DID WRONG...

I KNOW WHAT I DID WRONG! I NEVER SHOULD HAVE SPOKEN TO YOU YEARS AGO! I NEVER SHOULD HAVE LET YOU INTO MY LIFE! I SHOULD HAVE WALKED AWAY! I SHOULD HAVE TOLD YOU TO GET LOST! THAT'S WHAT I DID WRONG, YOU BLOCKHEAD!!

YOU ALSO PROBABLY SHOULD HOLD YOUR HANDS A LITTLE CLOSER TOGETHER...

SCHULZ

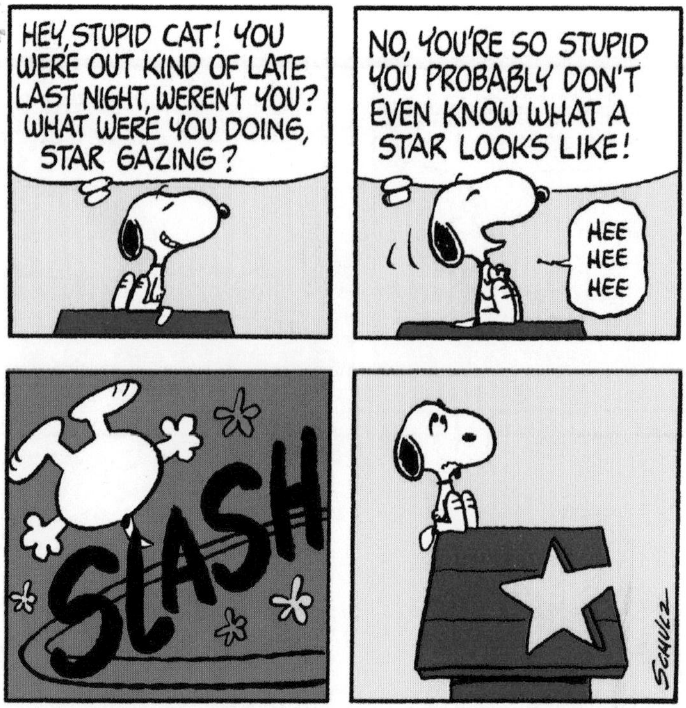
HEY, STUPID CAT! YOU WERE OUT KIND OF LATE LAST NIGHT, WEREN'T YOU? WHAT WERE YOU DOING, STAR GAZING?
NO, YOU'RE SO STUPID YOU PROBABLY DON'T EVEN KNOW WHAT A STAR LOOKS LIKE!
HEE HEE HEE
SLASH
SCHULZ

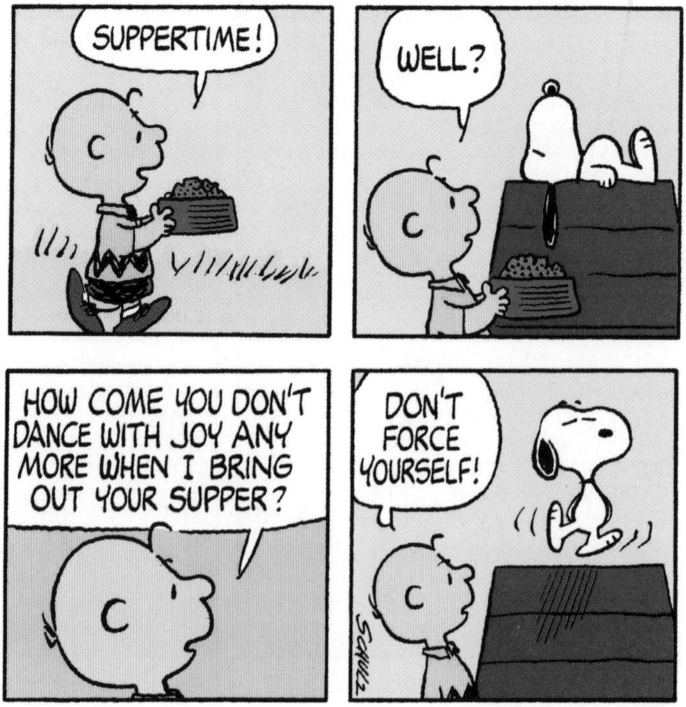
SUPPERTIME!
WELL?
HOW COME YOU DON'T DANCE WITH JOY ANY MORE WHEN I BRING OUT YOUR SUPPER?
DON'T FORCE YOURSELF!
SCHULZ

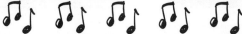

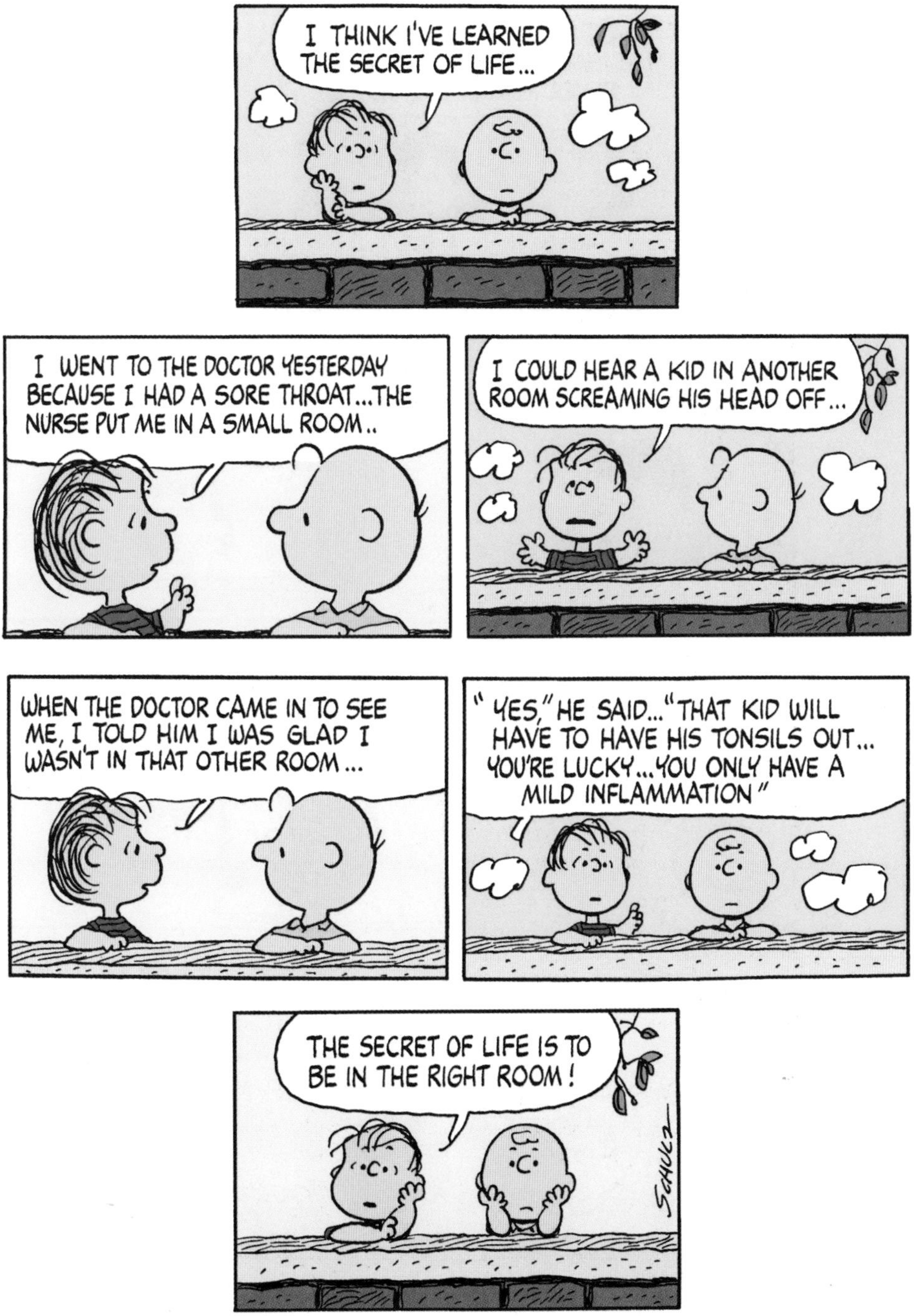
I THINK I'VE LEARNED THE SECRET OF LIFE...
I WENT TO THE DOCTOR YESTERDAY BECAUSE I HAD A SORE THROAT...THE NURSE PUT ME IN A SMALL ROOM..
I COULD HEAR A KID IN ANOTHER ROOM SCREAMING HIS HEAD OFF...
WHEN THE DOCTOR CAME IN TO SEE ME, I TOLD HIM I WAS GLAD I WASN'T IN THAT OTHER ROOM...
"YES," HE SAID..."THAT KID WILL HAVE TO HAVE HIS TONSILS OUT... YOU'RE LUCKY...YOU ONLY HAVE A MILD INFLAMMATION"
THE SECRET OF LIFE IS TO BE IN THE RIGHT ROOM!
SCHULZ

60

YES, MA'AM, I'M AWAKE! THE MOVIE? OH, YES, MA'AM, THE MOVIE WAS GREAT!

WHAT WAS IT ABOUT? WELL, UH... IT WAS... WELL, I THINK....

I DON'T SUPPOSE IT WAS ABOUT DONNY AND MARIE, WAS IT?

I'VE BEEN THINKING ABOUT YOUR PROBLEM, SIR

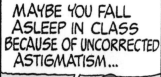

MAYBE YOU FALL ASLEEP IN CLASS BECAUSE OF UNCORRECTED ASTIGMATISM...

OH, SURE! YOU'D LOVE TO SEE ME WEARING GLASSES, WOULDN'T YOU, MARCIE?

SOME OF US THINK WE LOOK KIND OF CUTE WITH OUR GLASSES, SIR!

HAVE YOU MADE AN APPOINTMENT WITH AN OPHTHALMOLOGIST YET, SIR?

I DON'T WANT TO BE TOLD THAT I HAVE TO WEAR GLASSES, MARCIE!

YOU COULD BE SQUINTING AND NOT EVEN KNOW IT, SIR.. THAT CAN CAUSE EYE FATIGUE, AND MAKE YOU SLEEPY...

BESIDES, IF YOU WORE GLASSES, YOU MIGHT LOOK LIKE ELTON JOHN!

YES, DOCTOR...A FRIEND OF MINE SUGGESTED I COME TO SEE YOU...

WELL, I'VE BEEN HAVING TROUBLE STAYING AWAKE IN CLASS, AND SHE THINKS IT MIGHT BE BECAUSE OF MY EYES

AN EXAMINATION? YES, SIR...

HOW LONG DO I HAVE TO LIVE, DOC?

HEY, CHUCK, THIS IS GONNA CRACK YOU UP! ARE YOU LISTENING?

MARCIE HAS THIS THEORY ABOUT WHY I FALL ASLEEP IN SCHOOL ALL THE TIME...IT'S A WILD THEORY..WAIT'LL YOU HEAR IT...IT'S REALLY WILD...

HEE HEE HEE

WELL, MARCIE'S USUALLY RIGHT ABOUT A LOT OF THINGS..SHE'S PRETTY SHARP

DO YOU LOVE ME, CHUCK?

I CALLED HIM LAST NIGHT, MARCIE... I CALLED CHUCK, AND I ASKED HIM IF HE LOVES ME...

THAT STUPID CHUCK!! HE DIDN'T EVEN KNOW WHAT TO SAY!

I THOUGHT TALKING TO HIM ON THE PHONE WOULD HELP...

SOMETIMES, IF YOU TALK TO SOMEONE ON THE PHONE LONG ENOUGH, THEY'LL FORGET YOU HAVE A BIG NOSE!

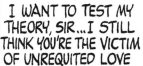

I WANT TO TEST MY THEORY, SIR... I STILL THINK YOU'RE THE VICTIM OF UNREQUITED LOVE

IF YOU JUST HAD SOMEONE TO KISS YOU GOODBYE WHEN YOU LEAVE FOR SCHOOL EACH MORNING, IT WOULD REALLY HELP...

WHERE AM I GONNA GET SOMEONE TO DO THAT?

TURN AROUND, SIR...

♡ SMAK ♡

YOU SEE, SIR, WE ALL NEED SOMEONE TO KISS US GOODBYE...

NO ONE SHOULD BE EXPECTED TO GO OFF TO SCHOOL, OR TO WORK OR TO JOIN THE NAVY WITHOUT SOMEONE TO KISS HIM GOODBYE!

IT'S JUST HUMAN NATURE...

WE ALL NEED SOMEONE TO KISS US GOODBYE

"JOIN THE NAVY"?

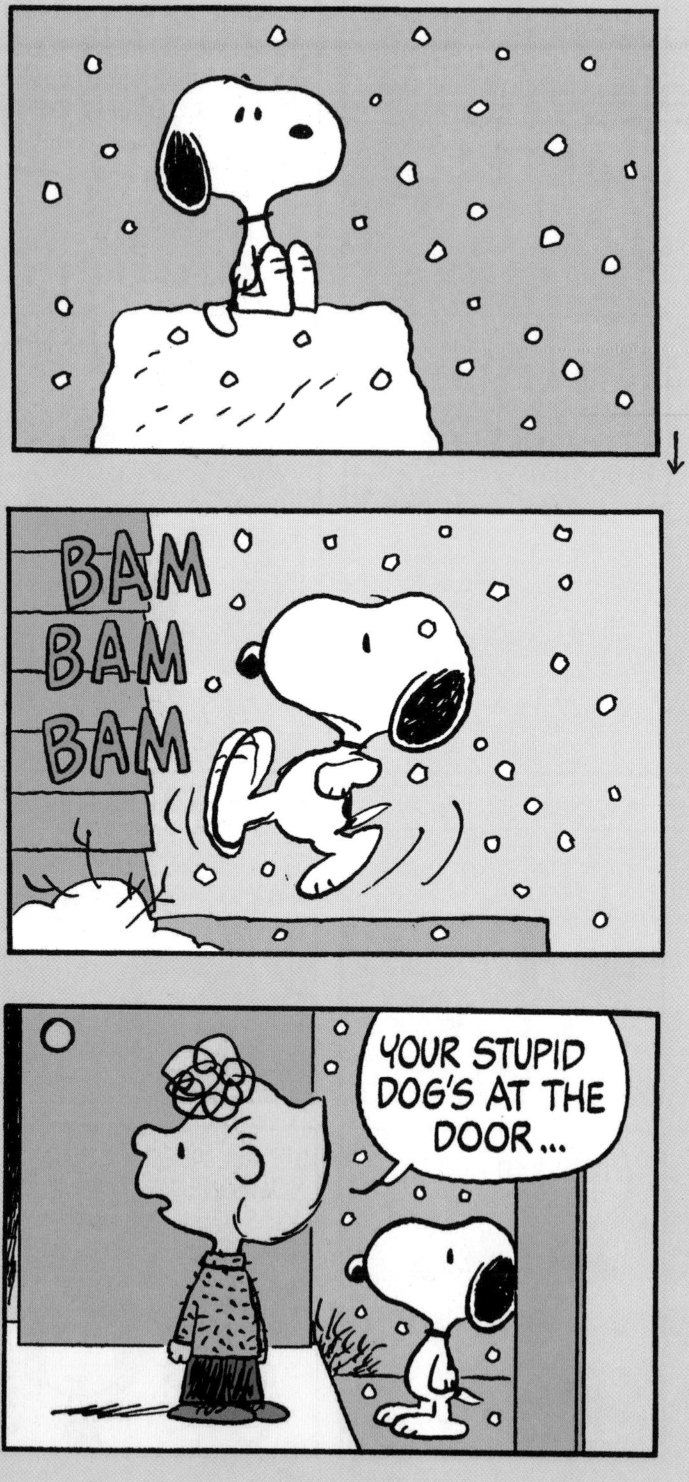
BAM
BAM
BAM
YOUR STUPID DOG'S AT THE DOOR...

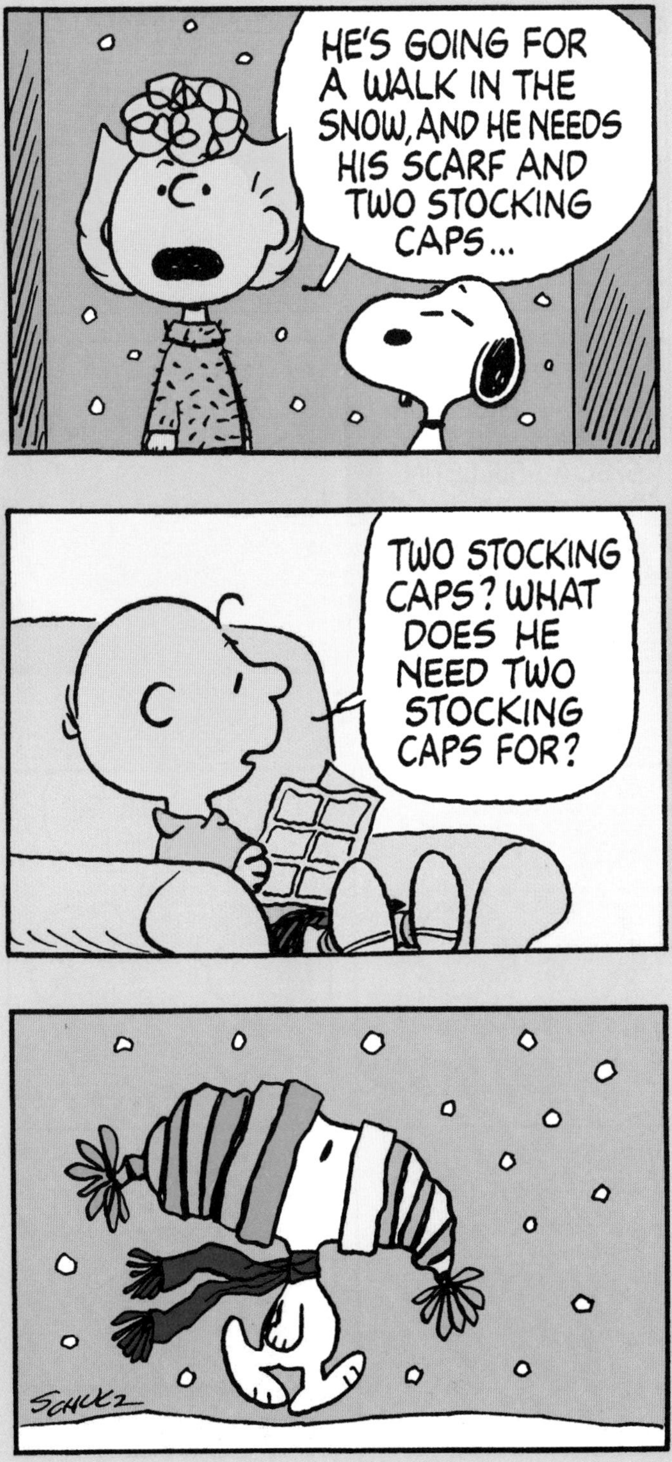
HE'S GOING FOR A WALK IN THE SNOW, AND HE NEEDS HIS SCARF AND TWO STOCKING CAPS...
TWO STOCKING CAPS? WHAT DOES HE NEED TWO STOCKING CAPS FOR?
SCHULZ

ONE MOMENT, PLEASE...

WE INTERRUPT OUR REGULAR PROGRAM TO BRING YOU THIS SPECIAL BULLETIN

IT'S A NICE DAY OUTSIDE

I'VE ALWAYS BEEN CRITICIZED

RIGHT FROM THE BEGINNING!

RIGHT FROM THE VERY FIRST DAY I WAS BORN...

THEY SAID I WASN'T RIGHT FOR THE PART!

I HAVE TO HURRY HOME TODAY, SCHOOL...WE'RE GOING TO VISIT MY UNCLE

I HAD AN UNCLE WHO WAS A COLISEUM

HE WAS A VERY PROUD BUILDING

WHEN THE HOCKEY FRANCHISE MOVED, IT BROKE HIS HEART

SCHULZ

I'VE NOTICED ON TV THAT SOME PITCHERS TALK TO THE BALL, CHARLIE BROWN.. HAVE YOU EVER TRIED THAT?

I ALWAYS TALK TO THE BALL WHEN I'M PITCHING...

REALLY? WHAT DO YOU TELL IT?

GOOD-BYE!

SCHULZ

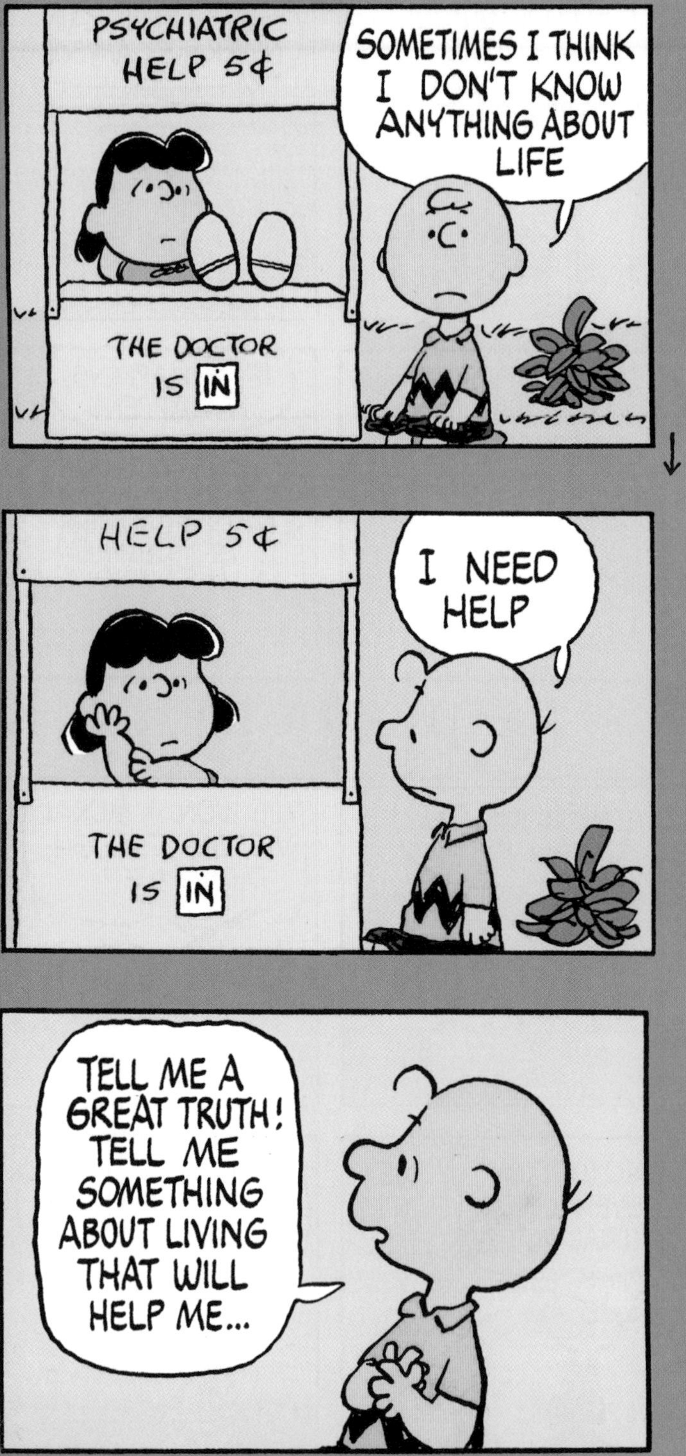
PSYCHIATRIC HELP 5¢
THE DOCTOR IS IN
SOMETIMES I THINK I DON'T KNOW ANYTHING ABOUT LIFE
HELP 5¢
THE DOCTOR IS IN
I NEED HELP
TELL ME A GREAT TRUTH! TELL ME SOMETHING ABOUT LIVING THAT WILL HELP ME...

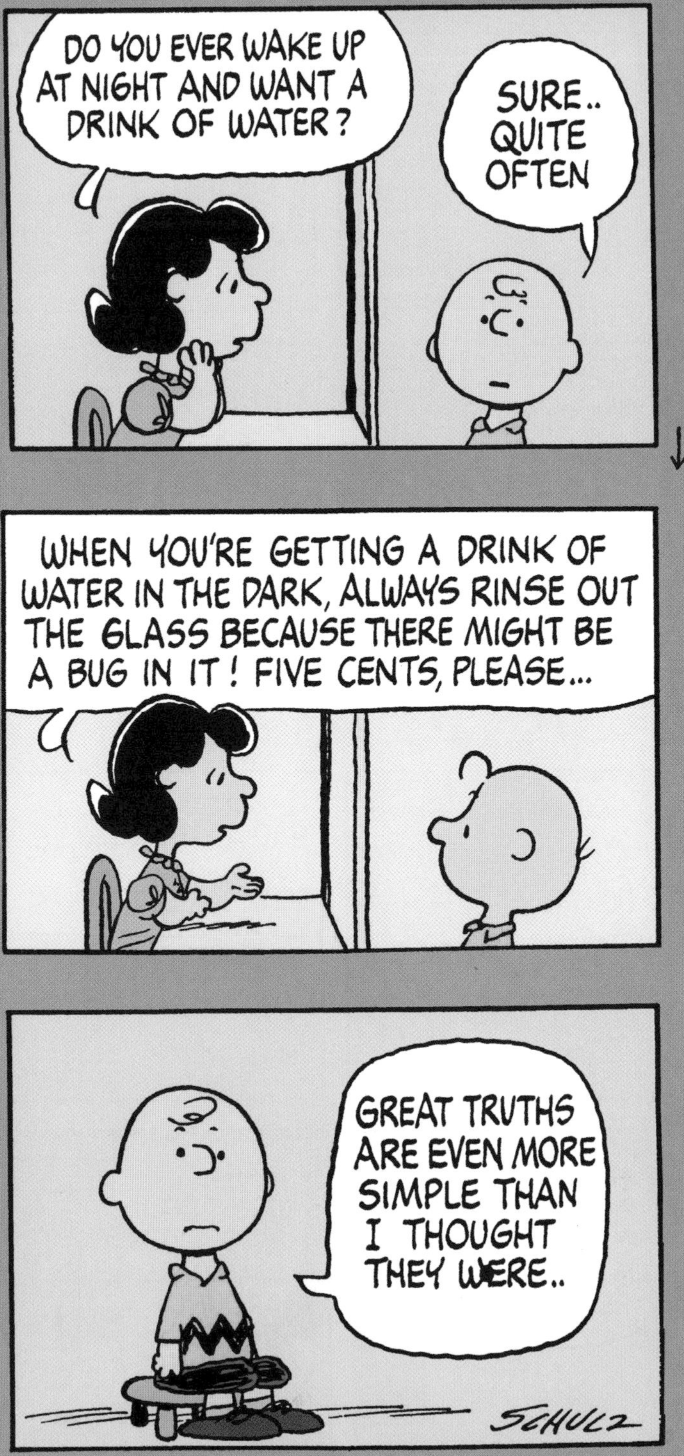
DO YOU EVER WAKE UP AT NIGHT AND WANT A DRINK OF WATER?
SURE.. QUITE OFTEN
WHEN YOU'RE GETTING A DRINK OF WATER IN THE DARK, ALWAYS RINSE OUT THE GLASS BECAUSE THERE MIGHT BE A BUG IN IT! FIVE CENTS, PLEASE...
GREAT TRUTHS ARE EVEN MORE SIMPLE THAN I THOUGHT THEY WERE..
SCHULZ

TRUE...FALSE...

TRUE...TRUE...
FALSE...TRUE...

MA'AM?

WHAT DO WE DO IF WE COME ACROSS A HALF-TRUTH?

HERE YOU GO!

THIS KIND OF DOG FOOD IS NO TROUBLE AT ALL

YOU JUST POUR IT INTO THE BOWL, ADD A LITTLE WATER AND STIR IT UP!

I'D RATHER BE WORTH A LITTLE TROUBLE

HOMEWORK? NO, MA'AM, I FORGOT TO DO MY HOMEWORK

I REMEMBERED TO GET OUT OF BED THIS MORNING...

I REMEMBERED TO EAT BREAKFAST AND I REMEMBERED TO COME TO SCHOOL

DO YOU GIVE CREDIT FOR THREE OUT OF FOUR?

HEY, MANAGER, THE COVER IS COMING OFF THIS BALL

MAYBE YOU SHOULD PUT SOME TAPE AROUND IT...

TAPE IT UP REAL GOOD SO IT WON'T COME APART AGAIN...

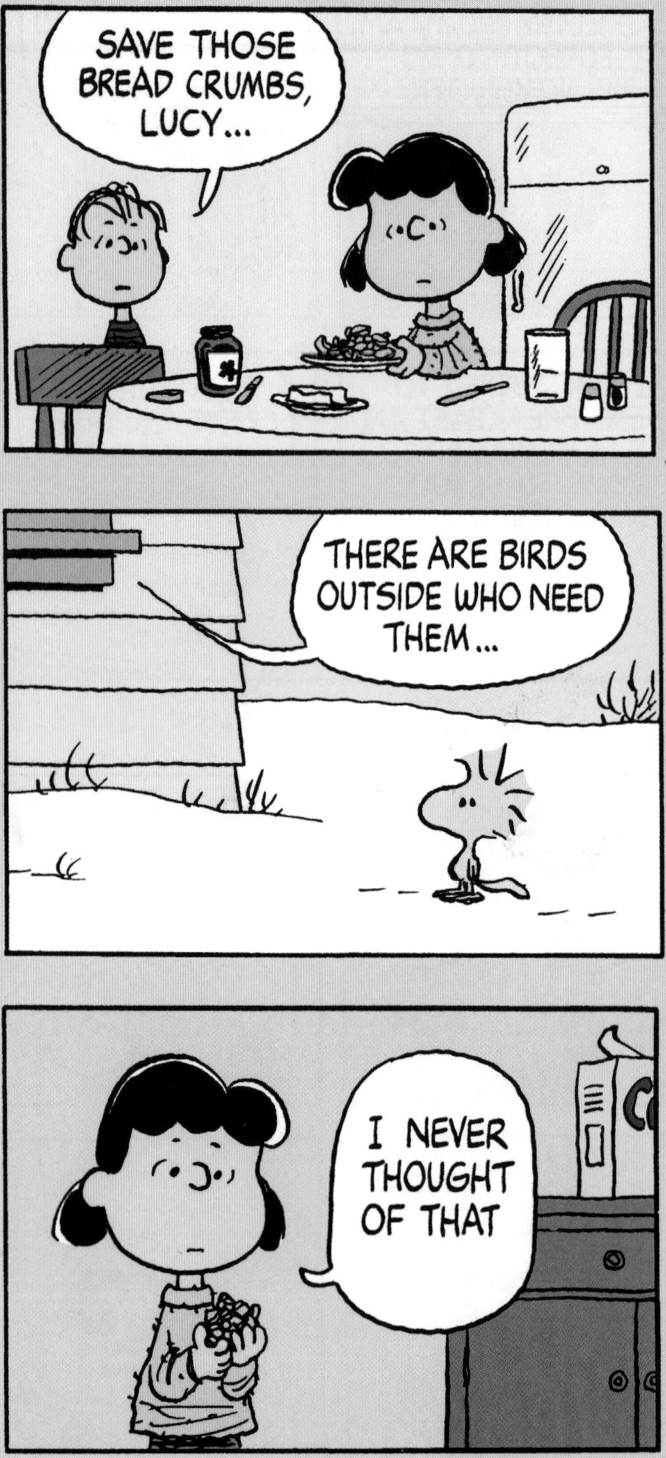
SAVE THOSE BREAD CRUMBS, LUCY...
THERE ARE BIRDS OUTSIDE WHO NEED THEM...
I NEVER THOUGHT OF THAT

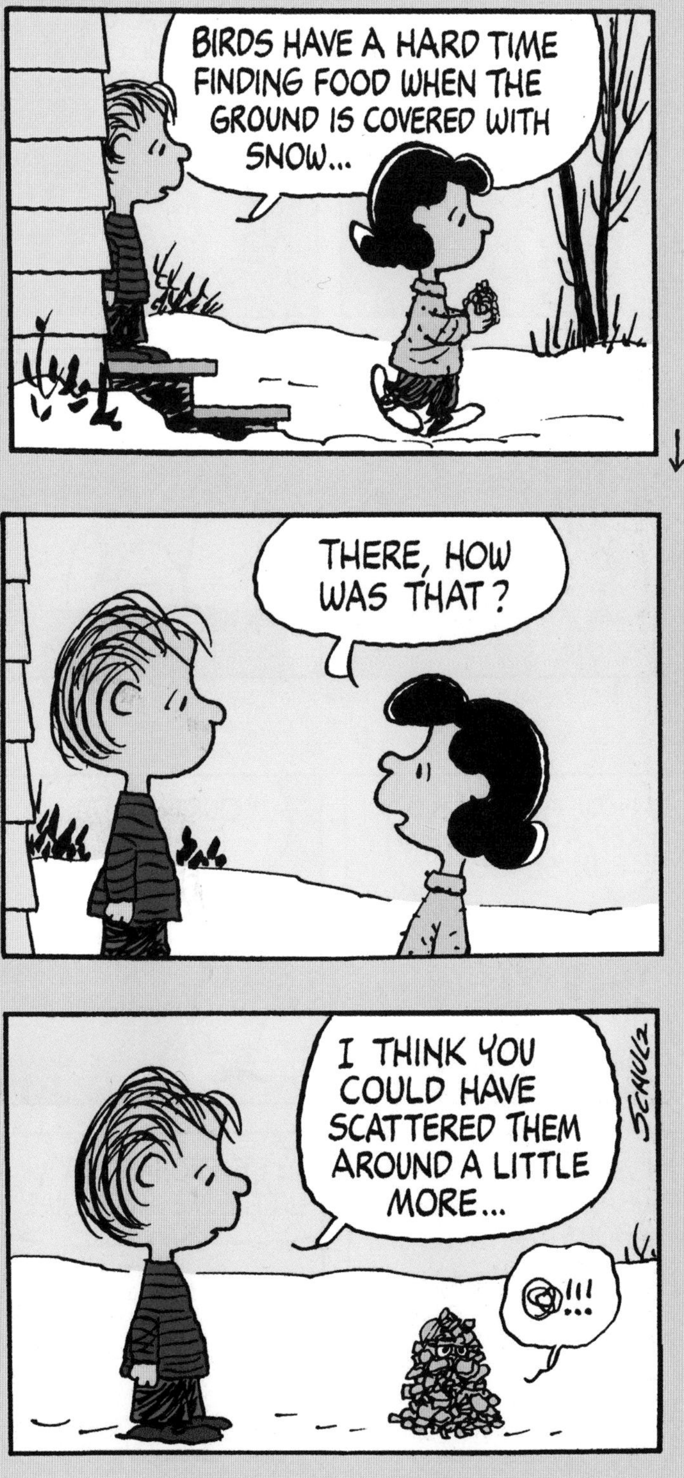
BIRDS HAVE A HARD TIME FINDING FOOD WHEN THE GROUND IS COVERED WITH SNOW...
THERE, HOW WAS THAT?
I THINK YOU COULD HAVE SCATTERED THEM AROUND A LITTLE MORE...
!!!
SCHULZ

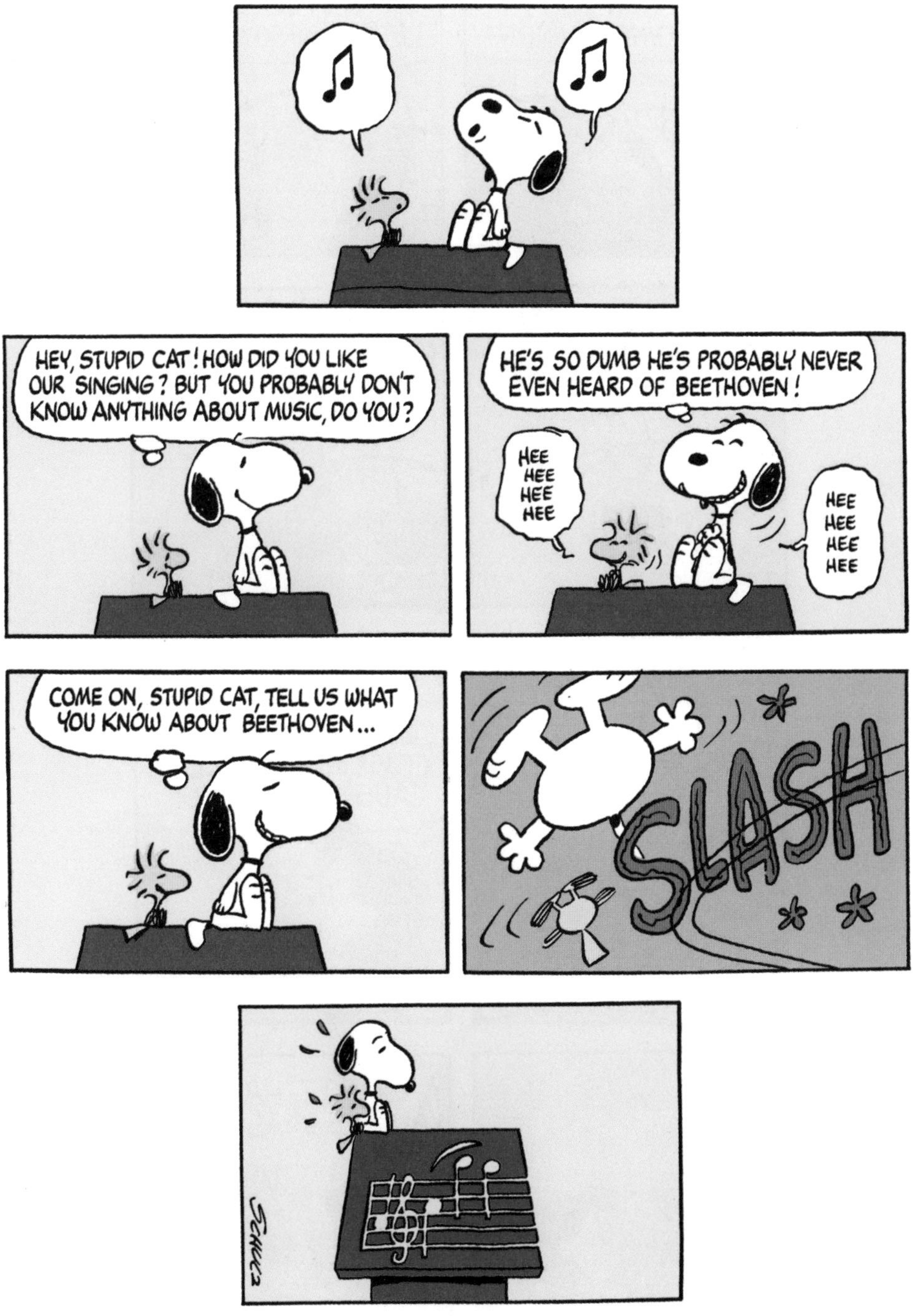
HEY, STUPID CAT! HOW DID YOU LIKE OUR SINGING? BUT YOU PROBABLY DON'T KNOW ANYTHING ABOUT MUSIC, DO YOU?
HE'S SO DUMB HE'S PROBABLY NEVER EVEN HEARD OF BEETHOVEN!
HEE HEE HEE HEE
HEE HEE HEE HEE
COME ON, STUPID CAT, TELL US WHAT YOU KNOW ABOUT BEETHOVEN...
SLASH

WHY DO WE FEET HAVE TO DO ALL THE WORK?

HOW ABOUT TOES? YOU THINK IT'S EASY BEING A TOE?

YOU GUYS ARE ALWAYS COMPLAINING.. WE EARS CAN HEAR YOU WAY UP HERE!

BESIDES, IT'S US LEGS WHO REALLY DO THE RUNNING...

ALL I KNOW IS, RUNNING IS HARD ON THE BACK... BACKS SHOULD BE HOME IN BED...

HOW ABOUT NOSES? I HATE JOKES ABOUT RUNNING NOSES!

LIPS ARE MADE FOR KISSING, NOT RUNNING...WE NEED MORE KISSING...

I'M HUNGRY!

HA! I KNEW THE STOMACH WOULD START COMPLAINING PRETTY SOON! WE ARMS NEVER COMPLAIN

THAT'S A LAUGH! IF IT ISN'T BURSITIS, IT'S TENNIS ELBOW! WE STILL SAY IT'S WE FEET WHO DO ALL THE WORK...

YOU THINK IT'S EASY BEING A FINGER?

HA! JUST TRY BEING AN ELBOW SOMETIME!

HOW CAN THE LONG-DISTANCE RUNNER EVER GET LONELY?

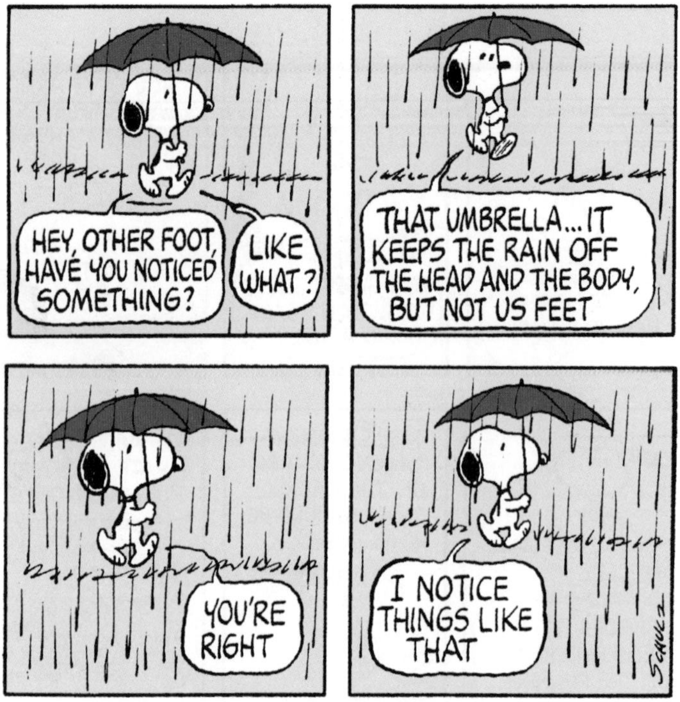
HEY, OTHER FOOT, HAVE YOU NOTICED SOMETHING?
LIKE WHAT?
THAT UMBRELLA...IT KEEPS THE RAIN OFF THE HEAD AND THE BODY, BUT NOT US FEET
YOU'RE RIGHT
I NOTICE THINGS LIKE THAT
SCHULZ

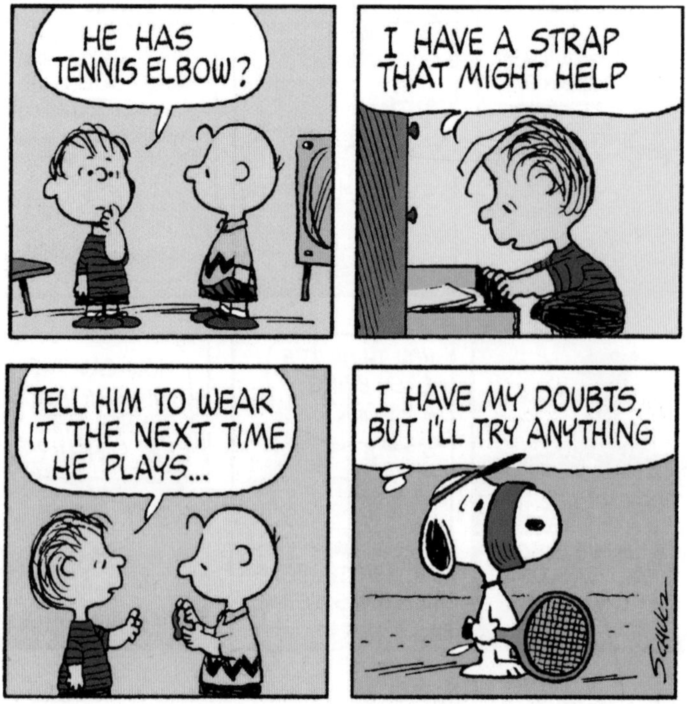
HE HAS TENNIS ELBOW?
I HAVE A STRAP THAT MIGHT HELP
TELL HIM TO WEAR IT THE NEXT TIME HE PLAYS...
I HAVE MY DOUBTS, BUT I'LL TRY ANYTHING
SCHULZ

100

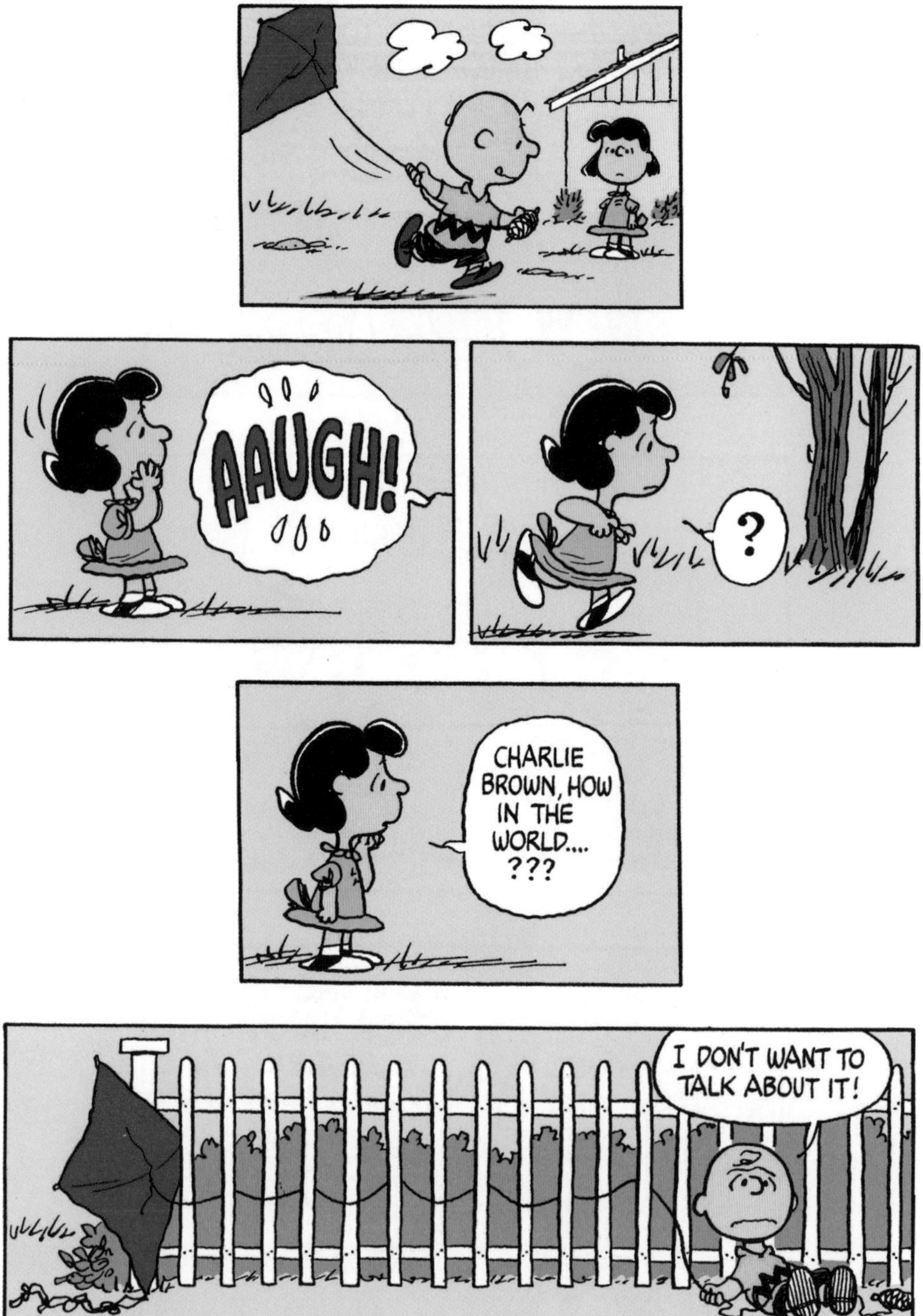
AAUGH!
?
CHARLIE BROWN, HOW IN THE WORLD.... ???
I DON'T WANT TO TALK ABOUT IT!

WHAT'S SO GREAT ABOUT LIFTING TWO ANGEL FOOD CAKES?

DON'T ASK ME WHERE I'M GOING! I'M GOING TO CAMP, THAT'S WHERE I'M GOING!

SO DON'T ASK ME!

WHY AM I GOING? DON'T ASK ME! BECAUSE I HAVE TO, THAT'S WHY!

SO DON'T ASK ME!!

HAVE A NICE TIME

IF WE BECAME LOST IN THE WOODS, HOW LONG COULD WE GO WITHOUT REAL FOOD?

I'LL BET WE COULD GO FOR A MONTH WITHOUT REAL FOOD

HOW ABOUT JUNK FOOD?

ELEVEN MINUTES!

EUDORA, ARE YOU CRYING? WHAT'S THE MATTER?

I NEVER WANTED TO COME TO THIS CAMP

BUT I'M NOT AS LONELY AS I THOUGHT I WAS GOING TO BE

I'M ONLY CRYING WITH ONE EYE

YOU'RE GOING TO TAKE ME FISHING? THAT'S GREAT! I DON'T KNOW ANYTHING ABOUT FISHING

WELL, WHAT WE'LL DO IS, WE'LL GO DOWN ON THE DOCK, AND SEE IF THERE ARE ANY FISH IN THE LAKE, AND THEN...

I SEE ONE!

YOU JUST PADDLE AROUND THERE AWHILE, AND I'LL EXPLAIN ABOUT THESE POLES...

OKAY, EUDORA, YOU FISH IN THIS PART OF THE STREAM, AND I'LL FISH DOWN THERE IN THAT PART...

I DON'T THINK THIS IS GOING TO WORK

WHAT'S THE TROUBLE?

EITHER THE STREAM IS TOO NARROW, OR MY LINE IS TOO LONG...

THANK YOU FOR TEACHING ME ABOUT FISHING TODAY, SALLY... I HAD FUN!

I EVEN WROTE HOME TO MY DAD, AND TOLD HIM THAT I CAUGHT A BLUE MARLIN...

GOOD GRIEF! HE'LL NEVER BELIEVE A STORY LIKE THAT!

HE'LL BELIEVE IT... HE WANTS ME TO BE HAPPY...

I CAN'T BELIEVE THAT I WAS AWAY FROM HOME FOR TWO WEEKS

I NEVER THOUGHT I'D MAKE IT... I THOUGHT I'D CRACK UP...INSTEAD, I FEEL AS THOUGH I'VE MATURED...

THERE'S YOUR MOTHER WAITING FOR YOU AT THE BUS STOP...

SO MUCH FOR MATURITY!

WELL, I SUPPOSE YOU HAD YOUR USUAL MISERABLE TIME AT CAMP...DID YOU HATE IT?

UNFORTUNATELY, NO! I MET A NEW GIRL THERE NAMED EUDORA

I HAD TO KEEP CONVINCING HER THAT CAMP WAS FUN...

MY MISERABLE TIME WAS RUINED!!

HEY, BIG BROTHER... I BROUGHT YOU A SOUVENIR FROM CAMP

HOW NICE...AN AUTHENTIC IMITATION ARROWHEAD!

IT WAS THE CHEAPEST THING I COULD FIND

HOW NICE...AN AUTHENTIC IMITATION SENTIMENT!

↓

OOOO! YOU LOOK SO CUTE LYING THERE, CHARLIE BROWN, WITH YOUR LITTLE EASTER TOES SPARKLING IN THE SUN
GET BACK IN CENTER FIELD WHERE YOU BELONG!
HOW CAN A PITCHER BE SO CRABBY ON EASTER?
SCHULZ

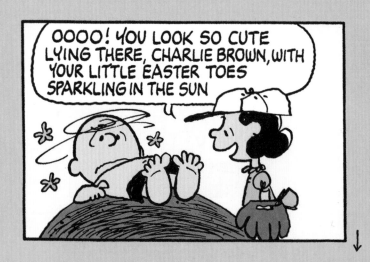

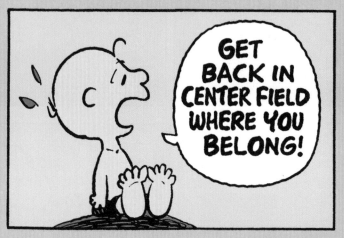

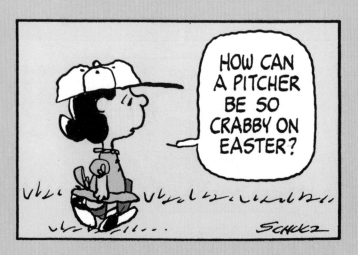

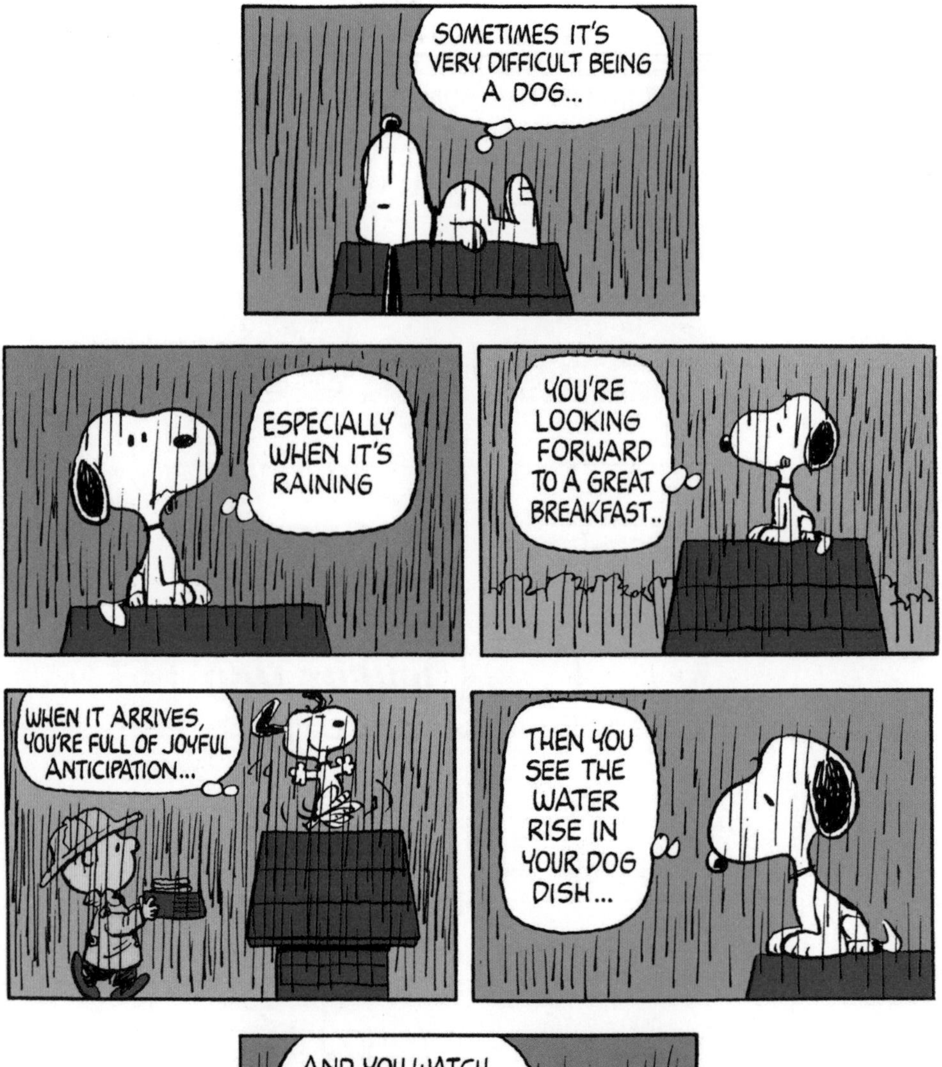
SOMETIMES IT'S VERY DIFFICULT BEING A DOG...
ESPECIALLY WHEN IT'S RAINING
YOU'RE LOOKING FORWARD TO A GREAT BREAKFAST..
WHEN IT ARRIVES, YOU'RE FULL OF JOYFUL ANTICIPATION...
THEN YOU SEE THE WATER RISE IN YOUR DOG DISH...
AND YOU WATCH YOUR PANCAKES FLOAT DOWNSTREAM!
SCHULZ

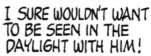

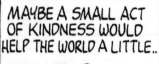

SPIKE JUST LEFT

SPIKE **LEFT**?

WE COULDN'T FIND A HOME FOR HIM AROUND HERE SO HE DECIDED TO HITCHHIKE BACK TO NEEDLES...

I LOANED HIM A FEW THINGS TO MAKE THE TRIP EASIER...

"AH, COLONEL HOGAN!"

KIDS AND PARENTS ARE ALWAYS ARGUING ABOUT SOMETHING

BUT KIDS HAVE THE ADVANTAGE

THEY CAN WEAR THE PARENTS DOWN

KIDS HAVE BETTER BENCH STRENGTH!

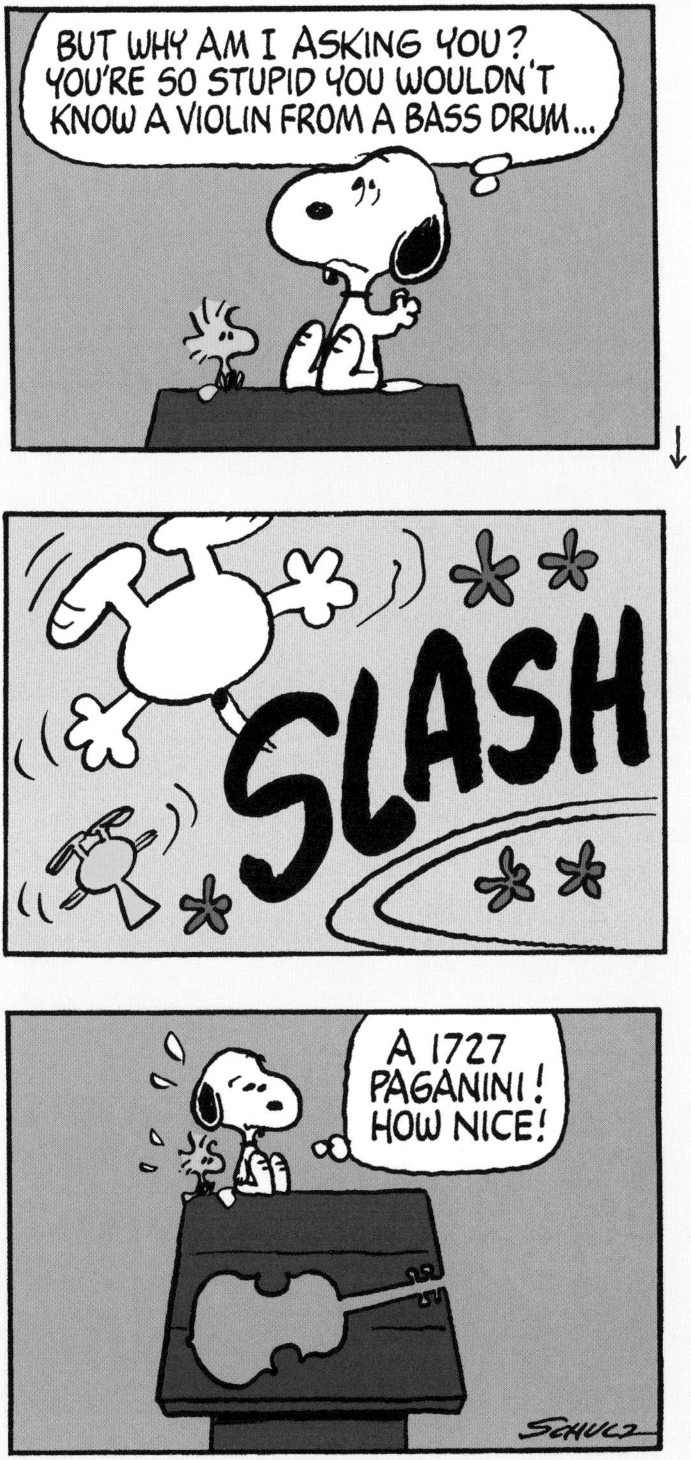
BUT WHY AM I ASKING YOU? YOU'RE SO STUPID YOU WOULDN'T KNOW A VIOLIN FROM A BASS DRUM...
SLASH
A 1727 PAGANINI! HOW NICE!
SCHULZ

I ALMOST BOUGHT YOU A BIRTHDAY PRESENT JUST NOW

I SAW THIS BOTTLE OF COLOGNE IN A STORE WINDOW, AND IT ONLY COST A DOLLAR...

I KNEW IT WOULD MAKE YOU HAPPY TO GET IT, BUT THEN I SAW SOMETHING THAT I KNEW WOULD MAKE YOU EVEN MORE HAPPY!

IN THE WINDOW OF THE STORE NEXT DOOR, THERE WAS A SALAMI SANDWICH WHICH ALSO COST A DOLLAR...NOW, I KNOW HOW CONCERNED YOU ARE FOR THE PEOPLES OF THIS WORLD...

I KNOW HOW HAPPY IT'S GOING TO MAKE YOU WHEN I BECOME A FAMOUS DOCTOR, AND CAN HELP THE PEOPLE OF THE WORLD

BUT IF I'M GOING TO BECOME A DOCTOR, I'M GOING TO HAVE TO GET GOOD GRADES IN SCHOOL...

AND TO GET GOOD GRADES, I'M GOING TO HAVE TO STUDY, AND IN ORDER TO STUDY, I HAVE TO BE HEALTHY...

IN ORDER TO BE HEALTHY, I HAVE TO EAT...SO INSTEAD OF THE COLOGNE, I BOUGHT THE SANDWICH...ALL FOR YOUR HAPPINESS!

I'M SO HAPPY I COULD CRY!

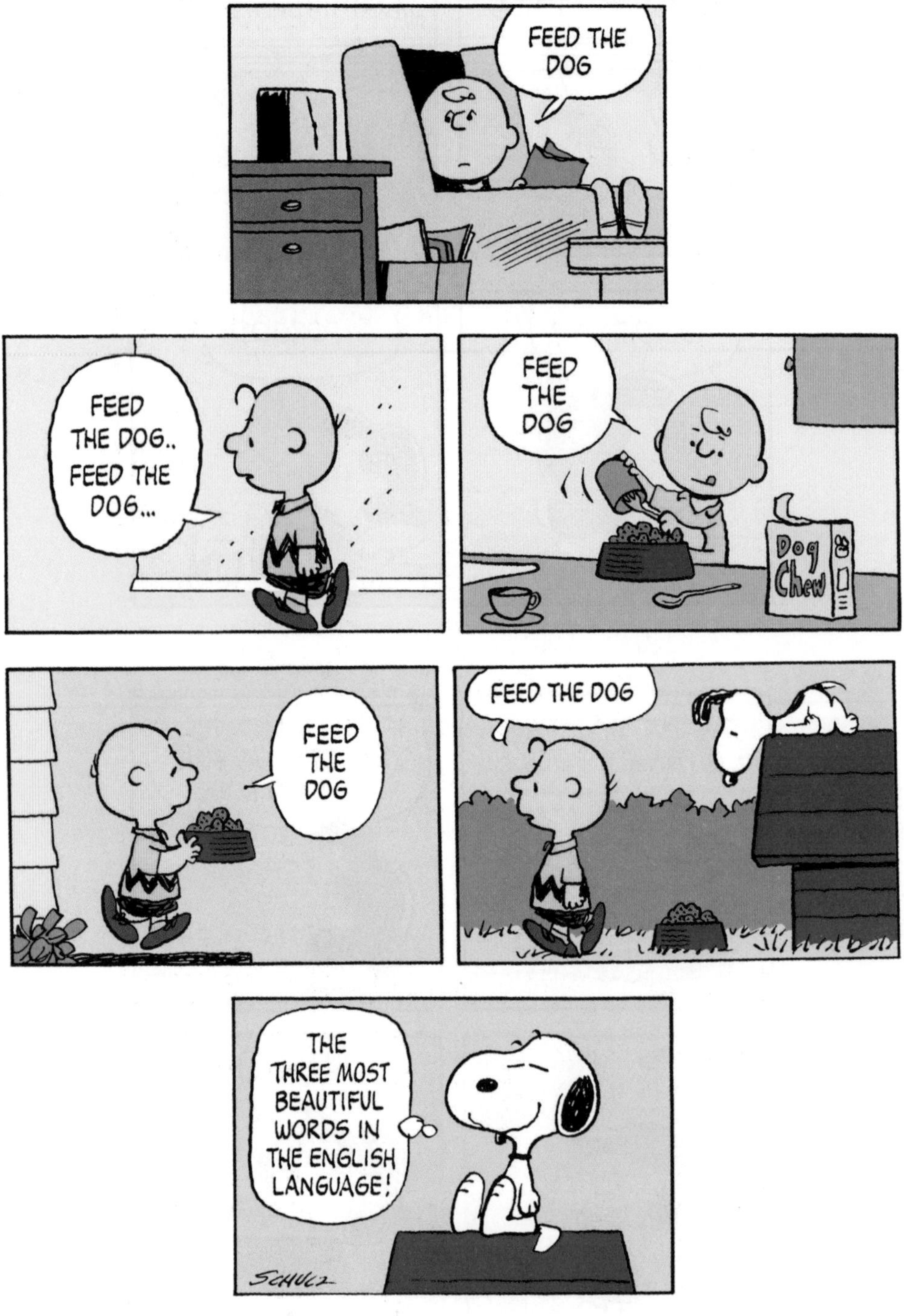
FEED THE DOG
FEED THE DOG.. FEED THE DOG...
FEED THE DOG
Dog Chew
FEED THE DOG
FEED THE DOG
THE THREE MOST BEAUTIFUL WORDS IN THE ENGLISH LANGUAGE!
SCHULZ

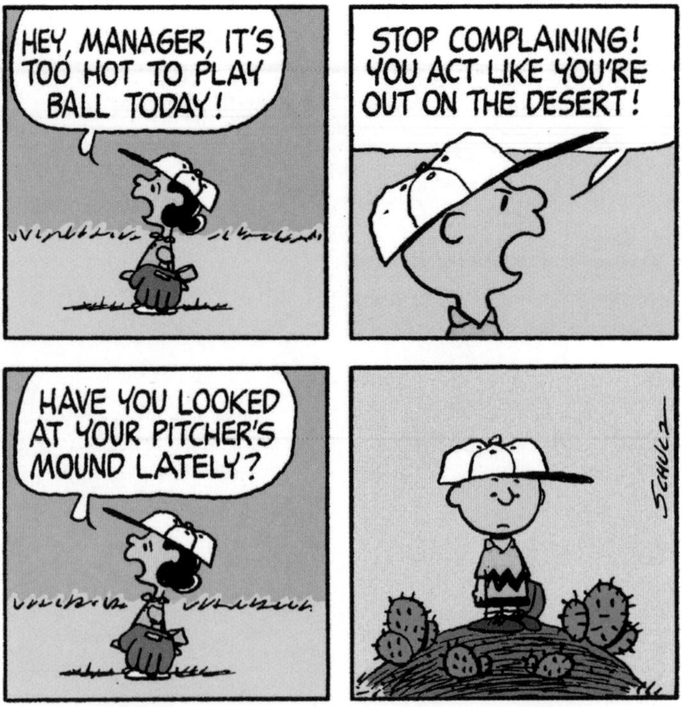
HEY, MANAGER, IT'S TOO HOT TO PLAY BALL TODAY!
STOP COMPLAINING! YOU ACT LIKE YOU'RE OUT ON THE DESERT!
HAVE YOU LOOKED AT YOUR PITCHER'S MOUND LATELY?
SCHULZ

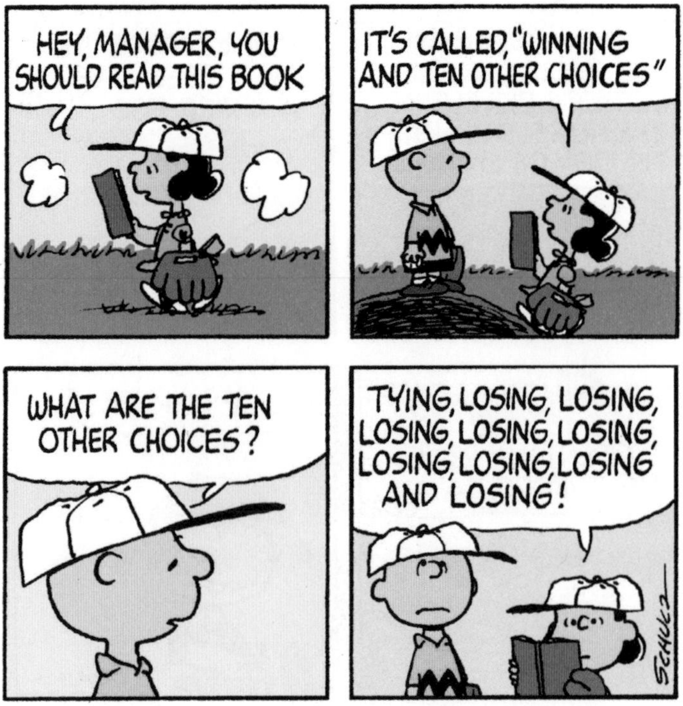
HEY, MANAGER, YOU SHOULD READ THIS BOOK
IT'S CALLED, "WINNING AND TEN OTHER CHOICES"
WHAT ARE THE TEN OTHER CHOICES?
TYING, LOSING, LOSING, LOSING, LOSING, LOSING, LOSING, LOSING, LOSING AND LOSING!
SCHULZ

WHERE ARE YOU GOING, BIG BROTHER?

WELL, I FINALLY GOT UP NERVE TO CALL THAT LITTLE RED-HAIRED GIRL, BUT I DIALED MARCIE BY MISTAKE, AND GOT A DATE WITH PEPPERMINT PATTY...

I THINK YOU'RE TOO WISHY-WASHY, BIG BROTHER

IT'S NOT A LOST ART!

IT'S A BEAUTIFUL EVENING

THE WARM AIR STIRS MEMORIES

I'LL BET IT BRINGS BACK THOUGHTS OF THE OLD POPPY HILL DAISY FARM, DOESN'T IT?

THAT'S DAISY HILL PUPPY FARM!!

BONK!

IF YOU'RE GONNA FOOL ME WITH A DROP SHOT, YOU'LL HAVE TO DISGUISE IT BETTER THAN THAT!

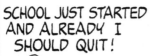

THAT HAS TO BE THE DUMBEST EXPERIMENT I'VE EVER SEEN!

WHY WOULD ANYONE WANT TO KNOW HOW MANY NOTCHES YOU CAN PUT IN A DOGHOUSE BEFORE THE ROOF FALLS IN?

IT'S CALLED "LIVE AND LEARN"

OR IS IT "LIVE AND DON'T LEARN"?

PSST! WAKE UP, SIR!

Z

I CAN'T LIFT MY HEAD, MARCIE...GIVE ME A LITTLE PUSH...

BONK!!

DON'T CALL ON ME FOR A WHILE, MA'AM... I'M HERE, BUT MY NOSE IS IN THE RECOVERY ROOM!

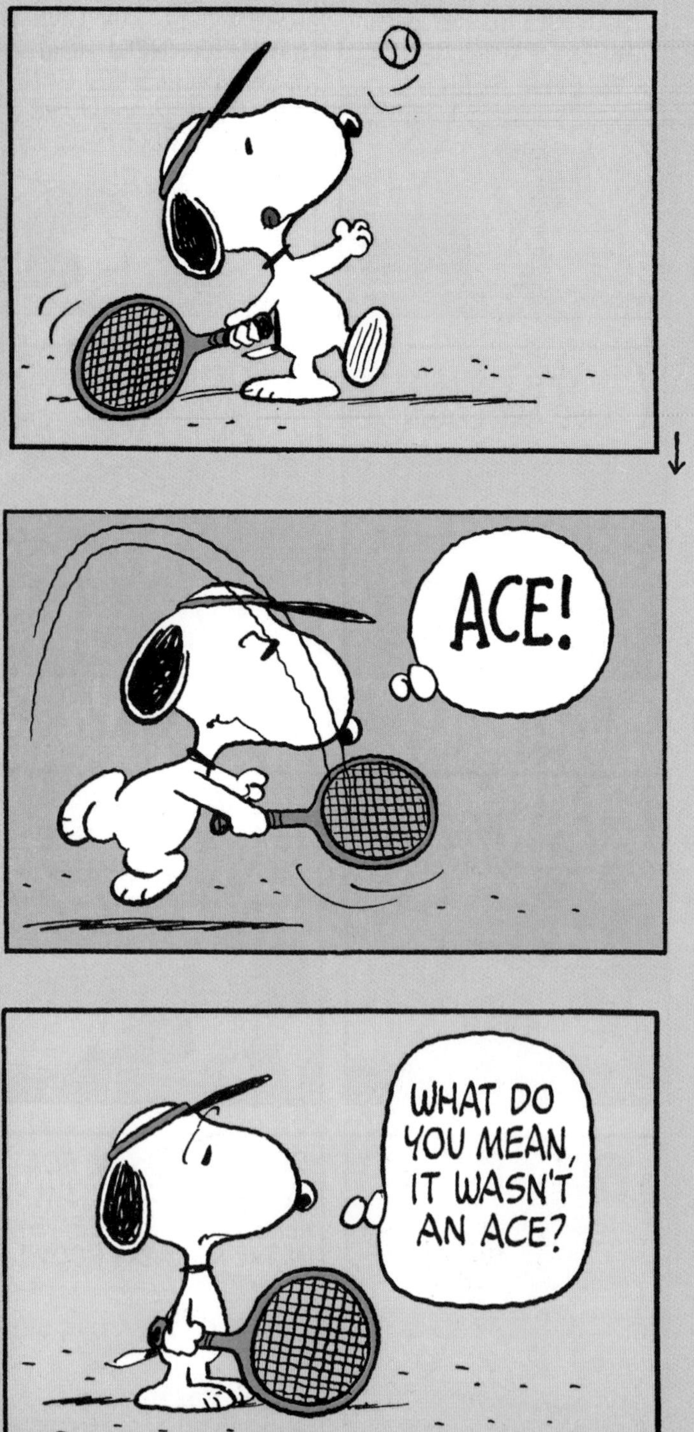
ACE!
WHAT DO YOU MEAN, IT WASN'T AN ACE?

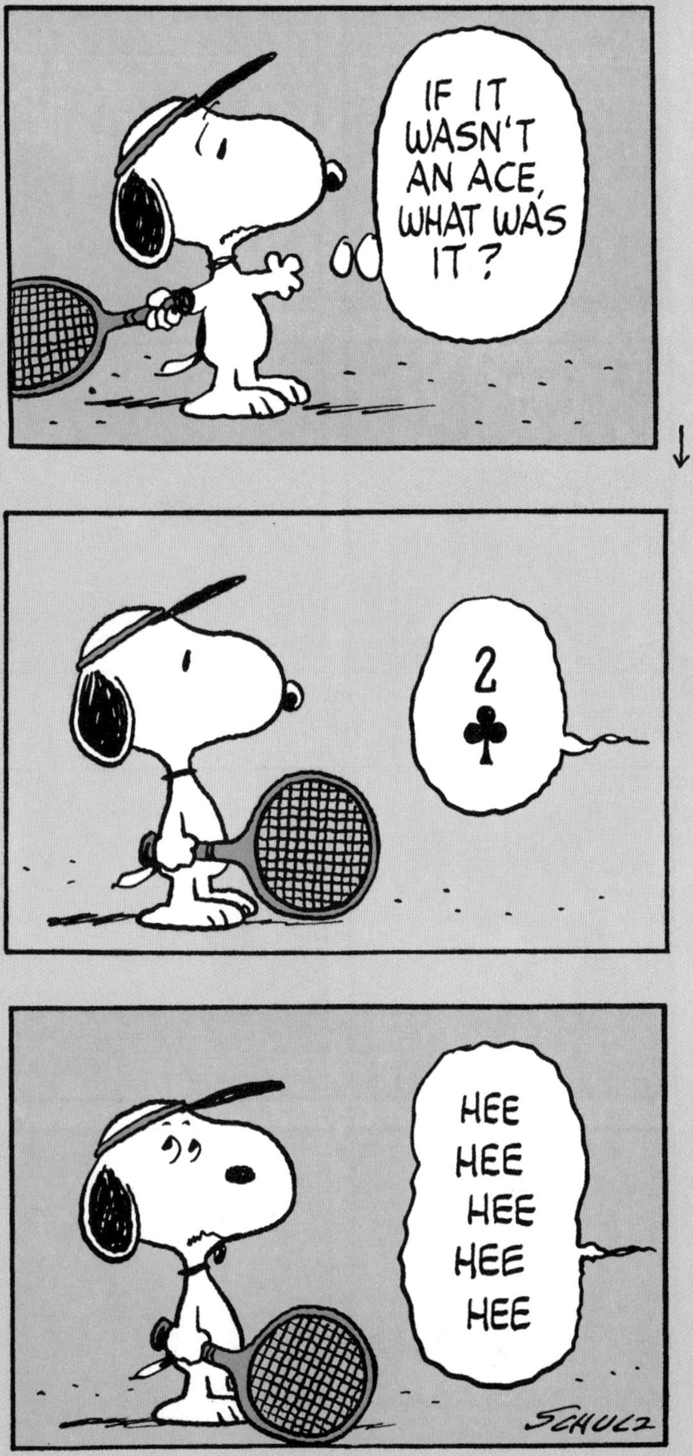
IF IT WASN'T AN ACE, WHAT WAS IT ?
2 ♣
HEE HEE HEE HEE HEE
SCHULZ

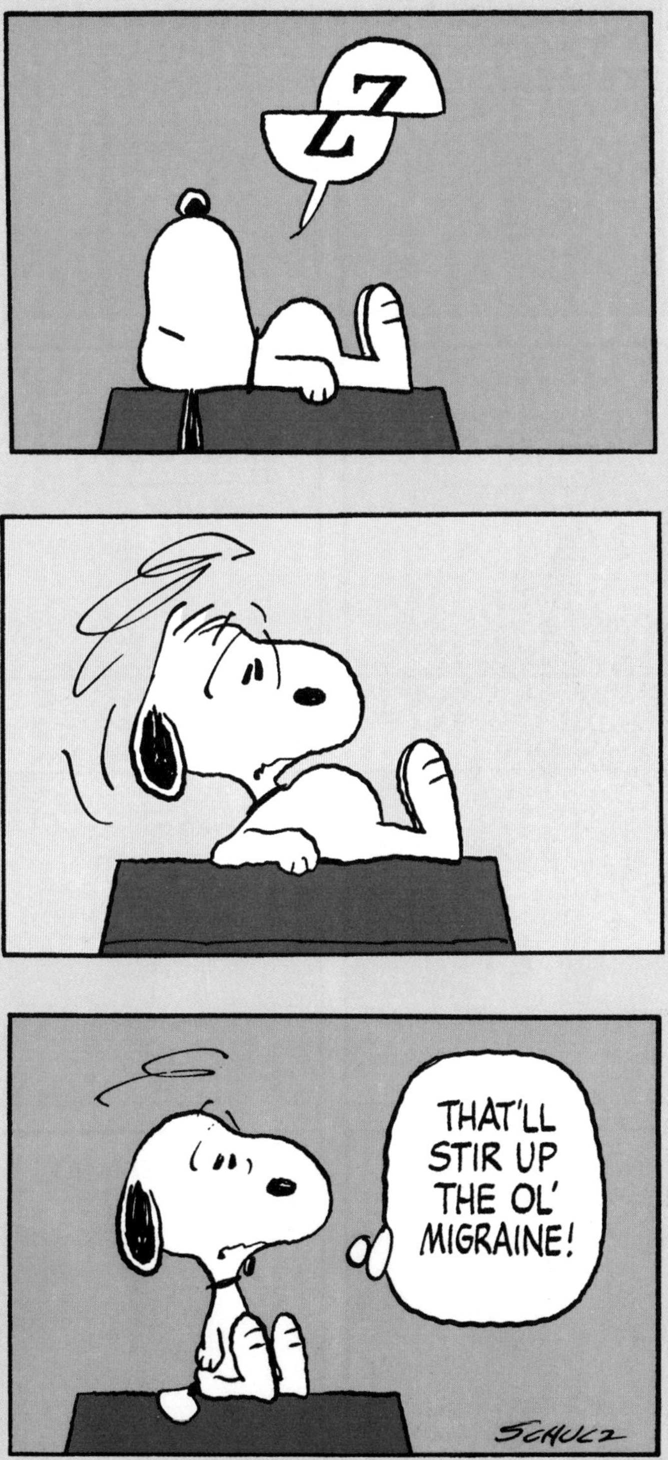
Z
Z
THAT'LL STIR UP THE OL' MIGRAINE!
SCHULZ

EUDORA! WHAT ARE YOU DOING HERE? THERE'S NO SCHOOL ON SATURDAY!

THERE ISN'T? THAT EXPLAINS EVERYTHING...

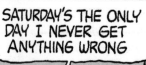

SATURDAY'S THE ONLY DAY I NEVER GET ANYTHING WRONG

I WONDER IF IT'S TOO LATE TO BECOME A DISCO...

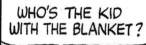

WHO'S THE KID WITH THE BLANKET?

THAT'S LINUS...HE'S MY SWEET BABBOO...

I'M NOT YOUR SWEET BABBOO!!

HE IS, BUT HE ISN'T, BUT HE IS!

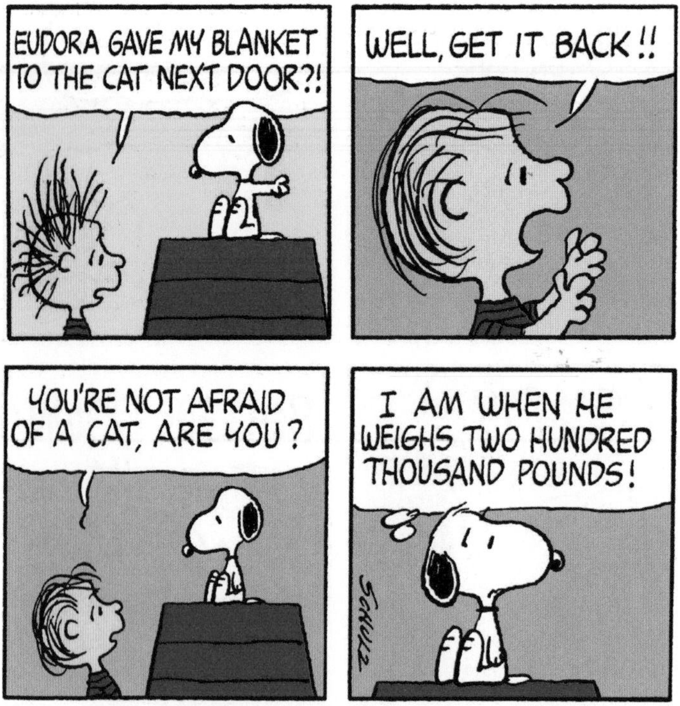
EUDORA GAVE MY BLANKET TO THE CAT NEXT DOOR?!
WELL, GET IT BACK!!
YOU'RE NOT AFRAID OF A CAT, ARE YOU?
I AM WHEN HE WEIGHS TWO HUNDRED THOUSAND POUNDS!
SCHULZ

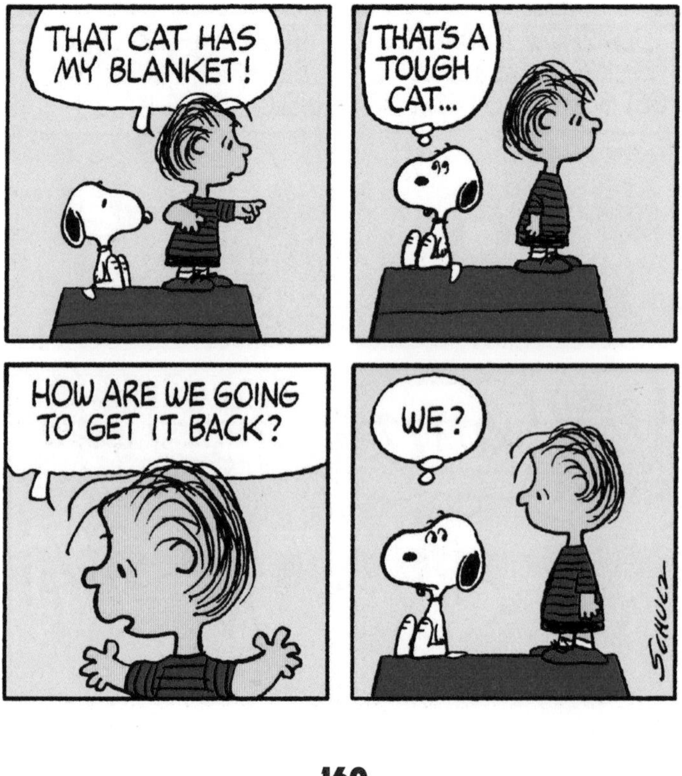
THAT CAT HAS MY BLANKET!
THAT'S A TOUGH CAT...
HOW ARE WE GOING TO GET IT BACK?
WE?
SCHULZ

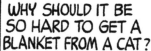

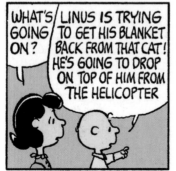

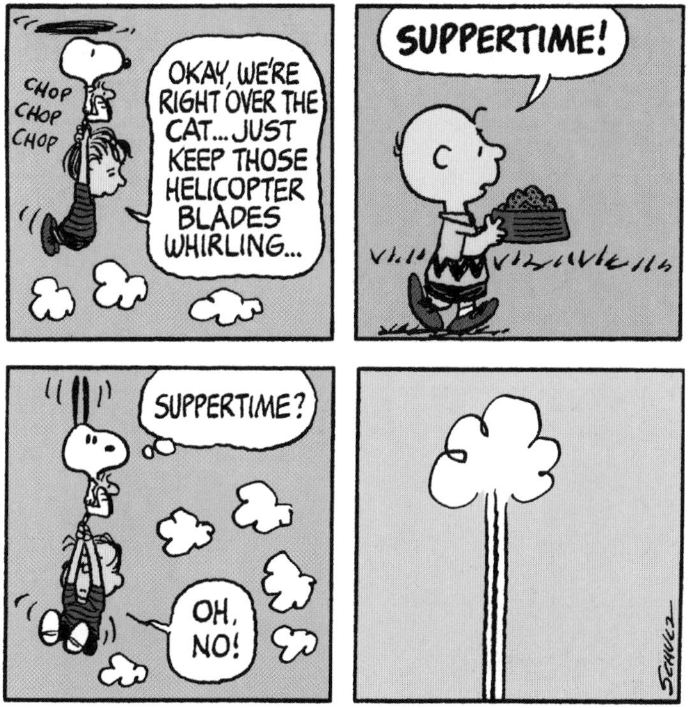
CHOP CHOP CHOP
OKAY, WE'RE RIGHT OVER THE CAT... JUST KEEP THOSE HELICOPTER BLADES WHIRLING...
SUPPERTIME!
SUPPERTIME?
OH, NO!
SCHULZ

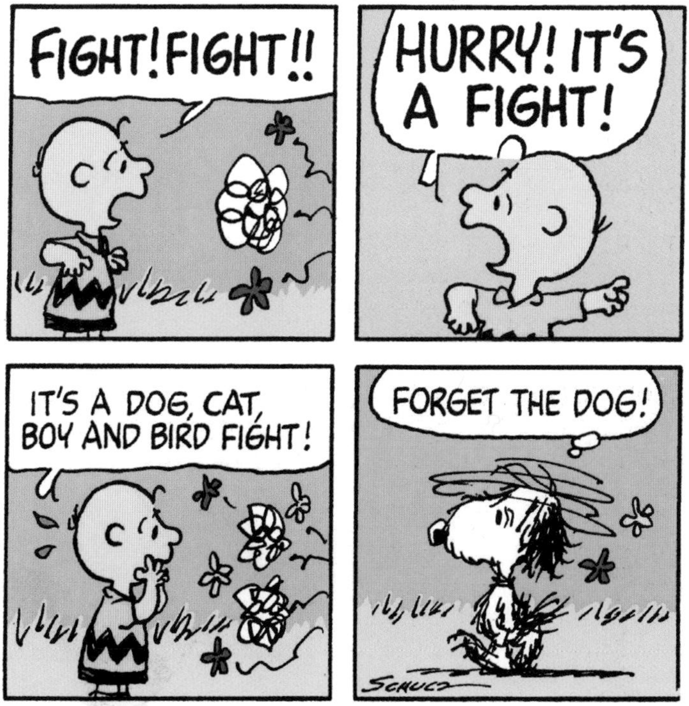
FIGHT! FIGHT!!
HURRY! IT'S A FIGHT!
IT'S A DOG, CAT, BOY AND BIRD FIGHT!
FORGET THE DOG!
SCHULZ

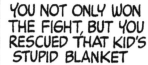

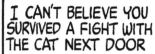

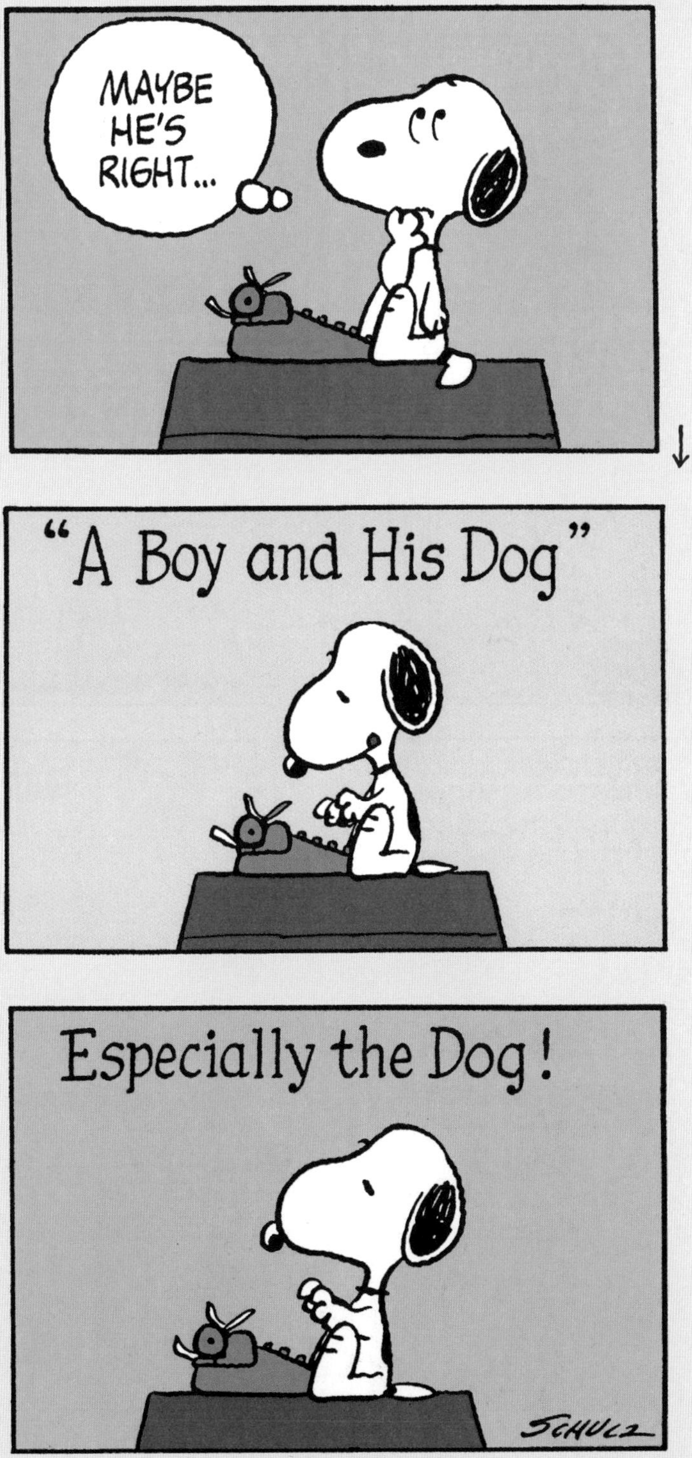
MAYBE HE'S RIGHT...
“A Boy and His Dog”
Especially the Dog!
SCHULZ

MORE TO EXPLORE! | **Featuring fun facts!**

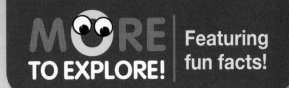

The *Peanuts* gang loves to dance! During his career, *Peanuts* creator Charles Schulz drew over three hundred strips that featured his characters dancing.

In the following pages, you'll see some famous examples of the *Peanuts* kids boogying down while learning a few of Snoopy's signature dance moves.

Special thanks to our friends at the Charles M. Schulz Museum and Research Center in Santa Rosa, California, for letting us share these with you!

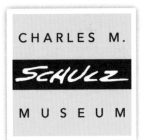

CHARLES M. SCHULZ MUSEUM

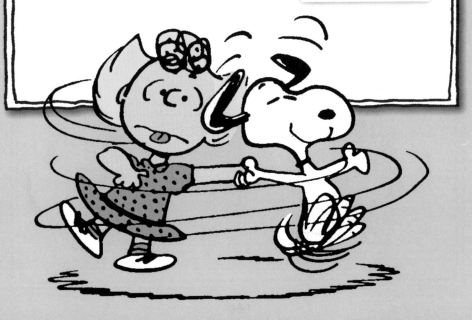

Snoopy's very first dance occurred in October 1952, only two years after *Peanuts*' debut. In the earliest years of the strip, dancing was portrayed fairly realistically, with one or more of the characters dancing for joy if they won a game or dancing while listening to music. Even Snoopy's dances were quite realistic, as he danced around on his back legs for a treat while the gang egged him on.

I'VE GOT TO ADMIT THAT THERE'S NOTHING LIKE THE 'POLKA' WHEN DANCED BY AN EXPERT..
SCHULZ

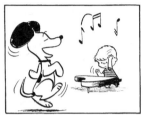

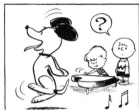

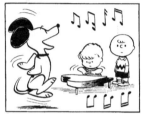

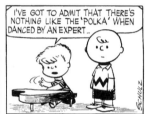

November 12, 1953

By September 1956, Snoopy was dancing purely for the joy of it. By that time, he looked less like a real pooch and more like the Snoopy we know and love today. In his popular "happy dance," Snoopy's love of life is easy to see in his body language: His ears fly up or to the side, and his "arms" open wide as if to embrace the world, while he drums his feet rapidly to the rhythm of the pure delight of being alive.

TO THOSE OF US WITH REAL UNDERSTANDING, DANCING IS THE ONLY PURE ART FORM!
SCHULZ

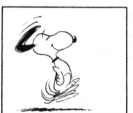

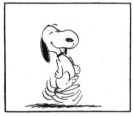

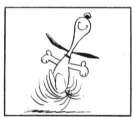

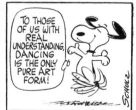

March 16, 1963

Although Lucy has partnered with Snoopy in some slow dances and some wildly exuberant ones, her patience with his dancing depends on her mood.

I DON'T UNDERSTAND YOU!
THE WHOLE WORLD IS COMING APART, AND YOU'RE DANCING!
I CAN'T HELP IT... MY FEET LOVE TO DANCE...
I HAVE AN OBLIGATION TO MY FEET!
SCHULZ

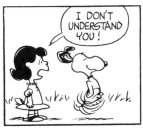

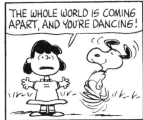

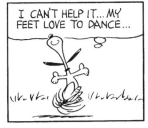

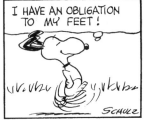

September 22, 1965

One of Snoopy's best-known dances occurs at suppertime. Snoopy's suppertime dance has become something of a standard, almost as iconic as his happy dance.

OKAY, YOU STUPID BEAGLE... IT'S SUPPERTIME!
SUPPERTIME?
OH, IT'S SUPPERTIME! SUPPERTIME, SUPPERTIME, SUPPERTIME!
YES, IT'S SUPPERTIME, THE VERY BEST TIME OF DAY!! OH, IT'S SUPPERTIME! IT'S SUPPERTIME!
I FEEL LIKE I'M FEEDING FRED ASTAIRE!

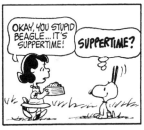

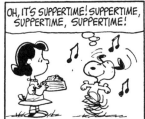

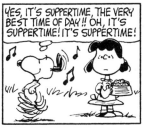

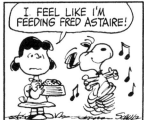

June 19, 1969

By the 1970s, *Peanuts* included story lines about dance fads and the gang's attendance at various social dances. You might have seen some of these in the *Peanuts* animated specials, with the characters showing off their signature moves.

December 3, 1970

In October 1978, Snoopy is seen wearing flashy disco attire and using cheesy pickup lines. To see the Snoopy disco strips, turn to pages 158–159 of this book!

In 1984, Snoopy also starred in the *Peanuts* animated special *It's Flashbeagle, Charlie Brown*, a reference to the 1983 movie *Flashdance*.

Snoopy may love the spotlight, but he's not the only *Peanuts* character who dances. Check out these strips featuring Woodstock, Peppermint Patty, Pigpen, Spike, and Charlie Brown.

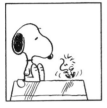

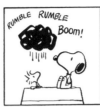

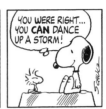

RUMBLE RUMBLE
Boom!
YOU WERE RIGHT... YOU CAN DANCE UP A STORM!

March 8, 1979

THIS IS SOME WEIRD DATE THAT CHUCK GOT FOR ME...
I MUST ADMIT HE CAN DANCE, THOUGH
WHAT'S YOUR SIGN, PIG-PEN? DO YOU COME HERE OFTEN?
WHERE DID HE GO?

February 14, 1980

HERE.. A LETTER FROM YOUR BROTHER SPIKE...
"DEAR SNOOPY, WELL, OUR CACTUS CLUB HAD ITS FIRST DANCE LAST NIGHT"
"ACTUALLY, THE DANCING WASN'T AS MUCH FUN AS I THOUGHT IT WOULD BE..."
OUCH! OOO! OW!! OUCH!

March 29, 1985

HI! MY NAME IS EMILY..WOULD YOU LIKE TO BE MY DANCE PARTNER?
WELL, SURE.. BUT I'M NOT VERY GOOD..
IT'LL BE EASY.. "SLOW, SLOW, QUICK, QUICK"
HOW ABOUT, "SLOW, SLOW, PANIC, PANIC"?

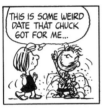

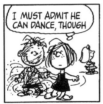

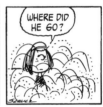

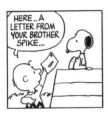

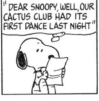

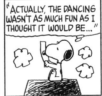

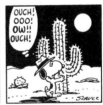

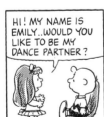

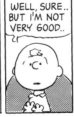

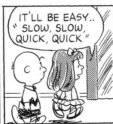

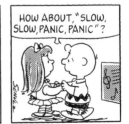

February 11, 1995

To see more classic *Peanuts* strips, learn about the art of cartooning, and take a virtual tour of the Charles M. Schulz Museum and Research Center, visit schulzmuseum.org.

About the Charles M. Schulz Museum and Research Center

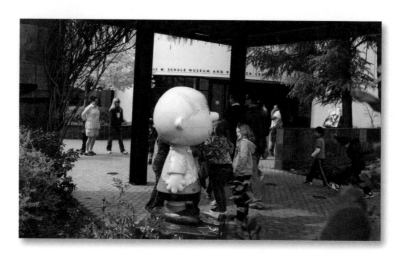

The Charles M. Schulz Museum and Research Center was designed as a tribute to the extraordinary talent of Charles M. Schulz. The Museum was created to share his legacy and genius with generations to come.

A tile mural over twenty feet high, Schulz's well-worn drawing desk, and a psychiatric booth are just some of the classics found alongside the largest collection of *Peanuts* artwork in the world. Laugh at original comic strips, explore in-depth exhibitions, watch animated *Peanuts* specials in the theater, and draw your own cartoons in the education room. The Museum features changing exhibitions, a re-creation of Schulz's studio, a life-size biographical timeline, and special programming. Learn more at schulzmuseum.org.

CHARLES M.
SCHULZ
MUSEUM

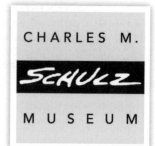

Peanuts is distributed internationally by Andrews McMeel Syndication.

Andrews McMeel Publishing
a division of Andrews McMeel Universal
1130 Walnut Street, Kansas City, Missouri 64106

www.andrewsmcmeel.com

www.peanuts.com

18 19 20 21 22 SDB 10 9 8 7 6 5 4 3 2 1

ISBN: 978-1-4494-9354-7

Library of Congress Control Number: 2018932253

Made by:
Shenzhen Donnelley Printing Company Ltd.
Address and location of manufacturer:
No. 47, Wuhe Nan Road, Bantian Ind. Zone,
Shenzhen China, 518129
1st Printing—7/23/18

ATTENTION: SCHOOLS AND BUSINESSES

Andrews McMeel books are available at quantity discounts with bulk purchase for educational, business, or sales promotional use. For information, please e-mail the Andrews McMeel Publishing Special Sales Department: specialsales@amuniversal.com.

Check out more *Peanuts* kids' collections from Andrews McMeel Publishing.

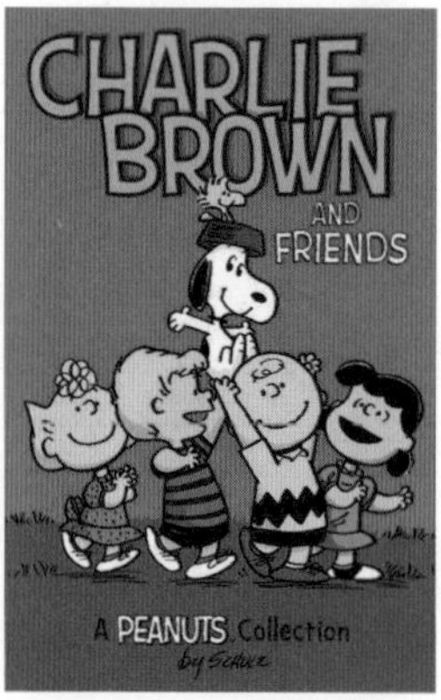
CHARLIE BROWN
AND FRIENDS
A PEANUTS Collection
by Schulz

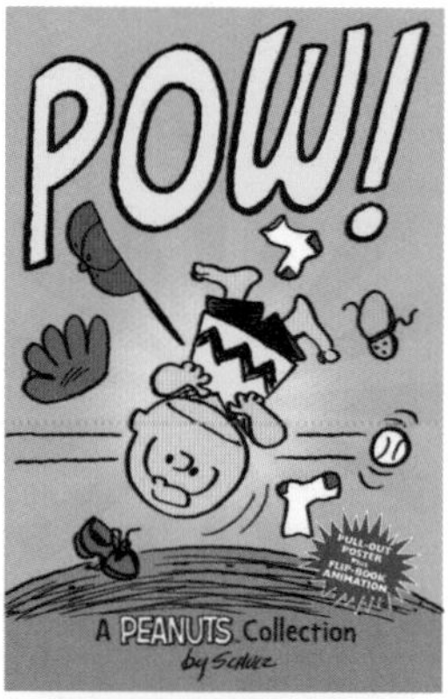
POW!
A PEANUTS Collection
by Schulz

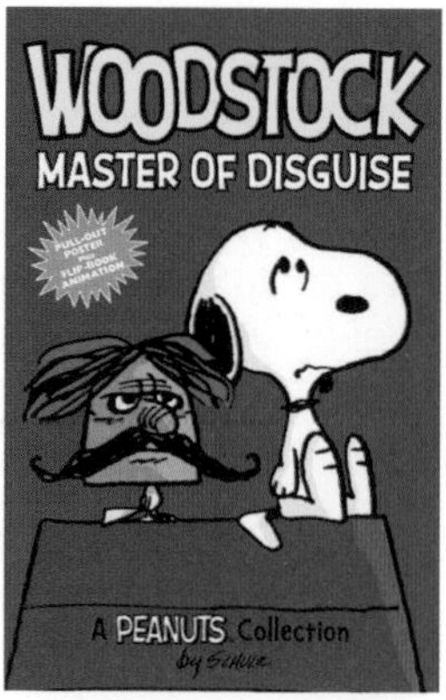
WOODSTOCK
MASTER OF DISGUISE
A PEANUTS Collection
by Schulz

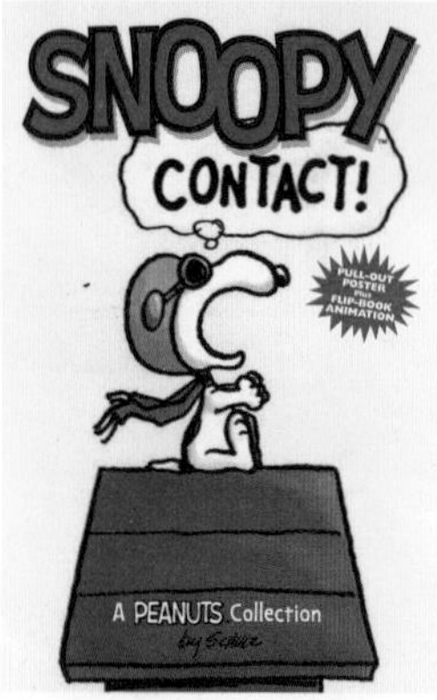
SNOOPY
CONTACT!
A PEANUTS Collection
by Schulz

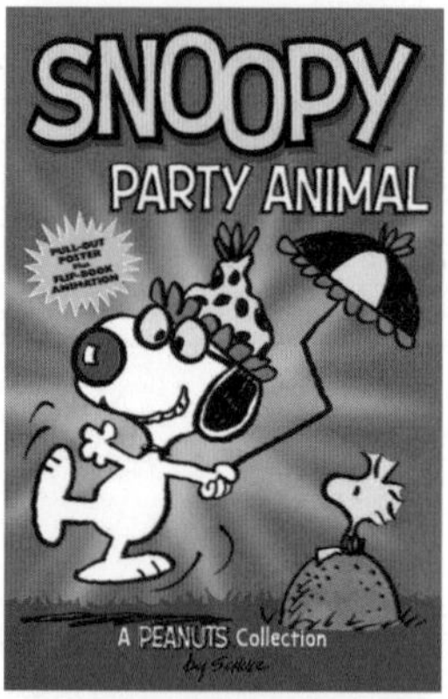
SNOOPY
PARTY ANIMAL
A PEANUTS Collection
by Schulz

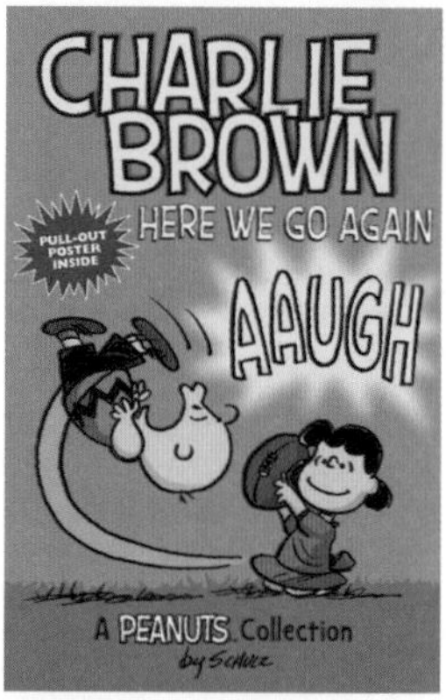
CHARLIE BROWN
PULL-OUT POSTER INSIDE
HERE WE GO AGAIN
AAUGH
A PEANUTS Collection
by Schulz

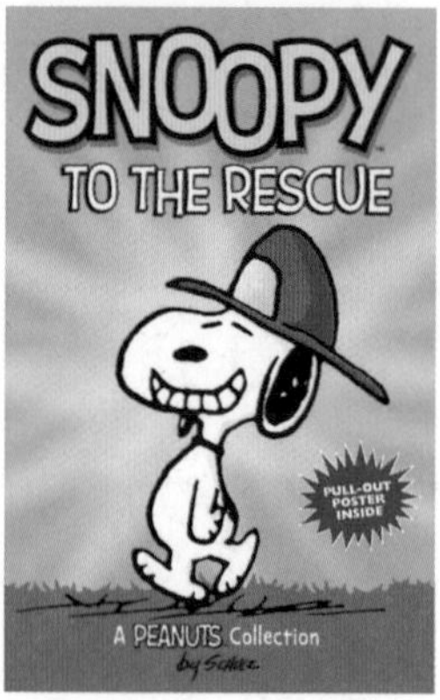
SNOOPY
TO THE RESCUE
PULL-OUT POSTER INSIDE
A PEANUTS Collection
by Schulz

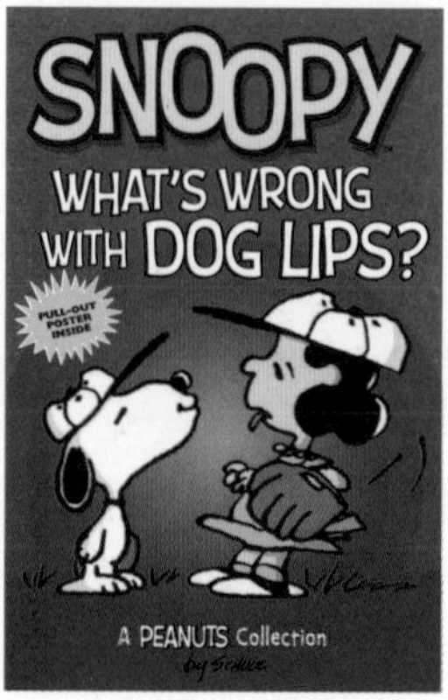
SNOOPY
WHAT'S WRONG WITH DOG LIPS?
PULL-OUT POSTER INSIDE
A PEANUTS Collection
by Schulz

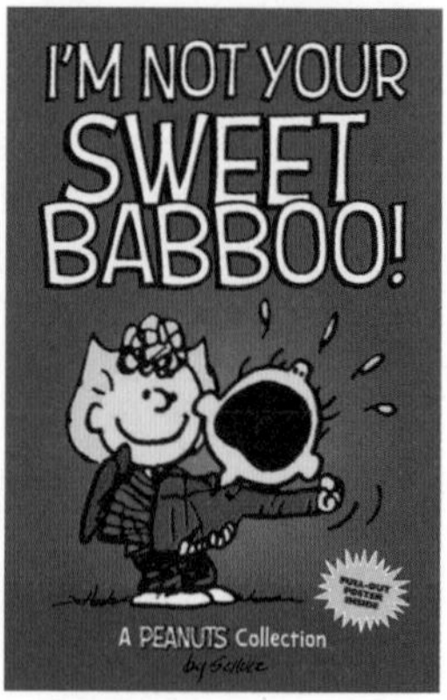
I'M NOT YOUR SWEET BABBOO!
A PEANUTS Collection
by Schulz